By

Dino Brancato

Table of Contents

Acknowledgements

I would first and foremost like to thank my dear friend Diana Martin who helped me come up with the title for the book. I would also like to thank Alissa, Tina, Annie and Brian for the great work they do.

Next I would like to thank my family and friends for their support and encouragement and of course you the reader for buying this book.

Forward

Do strange creature's really exist in the world?

Most scientists would say it's not likely. But believers point to interesting evidence such as unexplained footprints, photographs of unidentified animals, and audio tapes of unknown beastly sounds, all of which defy the understanding of current science.

Most often the only proof we have that we share this world with creepy creatures is the thousands of sightings reported by people of all ages and backgrounds. Usually witnesses reveal what they saw to their local police or sheriff's department. This suggests that they are telling the truth at least they see it because most people don't make false police reports, which is a crime. However, an untold number of sightings probably are never reported to the authorities. Often witnesses won't make an official report because they are afraid they will be laughed at if they say they've seen a monster.

So do strange creatures exist in the world? After reading in this book the accounts of such monsters as Bigfoot, Chupacabra, and Mothman, you can make up your own mind.

Chapter 1: Cryptozoology

Cryptozoology (from Greek κρυπτός, kriptos, "hidden" + zoology; literally, "study of hidden animals") is the study of and search for animals which fall outside of contemporary zoological catalogs. It consists of two primary fields of research. The first is the search for living examples of animals taxonomically identified through fossil records which are considered to be extinct. The second is the search for animals that fall outside of taxonomic records due to a lack of empirical evidence, but for which anecdotal evidence exists in the form of myths, legends, or undocumented sightings. A subset of the first field is the search for "out of place animals," such as Phantom cats.

Those involved in cryptozoological study are known as "cryptozoologists"; the animals they study are often referred to as "cryptids", a term coined by John Wall in 1983. Because cryptozoologists do not typically follow the scientific method and devote a substantial portion of their efforts to investigations of animals that most scientists believe are unlikely to exist, cryptozoology has received little attention from the scientific community. In 2004, however, paleoanthropologist Henry Gee, a senior editor of the leading journal

Nature argued that cryptozoology was of legitimate scientific value and could "come in from the cold."

Overview

Invention of the term "cryptozoology" is often attributed to zoologist Bernard Heuvelmans, though Heuvelmans attributes coinage of the term to the late Scottish explorer and adventurer Ivan T. Sanderson. Heuvelmans' 1955 book On the Track of Unknown Animals traces the scholarly origins of the discipline to Anthonie Cornelis Oudemans and his 1892 study, The Great Sea Serpent.

Heuvelmans argued that cryptozoology should be undertaken with scientific rigor, but with an open-minded, interdisciplinary approach. He also stressed that attention should be given to local, urban and folkloric sources regarding such creatures, arguing that while often layered in unlikely and fantastic elements, folktales can have small grains of truth and important information regarding undiscovered organisms. Loren Coleman, a modern popularizer of cryptozoology, has chronicled the history and personalities of cryptozoology in his books.

Another notable book on the subject is Willy Ley's Exotic Zoology (1959). Ley was best known for his writings on rocketry and related topics, but he was trained in paleontology, and wrote a number of books about animals. Ley's collection Exotic Zoology is of some interest to cryptozoology, as he discusses the Yeti and sea serpents, as well as relict dinosaurs. The book entertains the possibility that some legendary creatures (like the sirrush, the unicorn or the cyclops) might be based on actual animals, through misinterpretation of the animals and/or their remains. Also notable is the work of British zoologist and cryptozoologist Karl Shuker, who has published 12 books and countless articles on numerous cryptozoological subjects since the mid-1980s. Prominent cryptozoological organizations such as the the International Society of Cryptozoology and the Center for Fortean Zoology have attempted to apply a degree of scientific rigor to their work.

Relationship with mainstream science

Discoveries of previously unknown animals are often subject to great attention, but cryptozoology has seen relatively little interest from mainstream scientists. As historian Mike Dash notes, few scientists doubt there are thousands of unknown animals, particularly invertebrates, awaiting discovery; however, cryptozoologists are largely uninterested in researching and cataloging newly-discovered species of ants or beetles, instead focusing their efforts towards "more elusive" creatures that have often defied decades of work aimed at confirming their existence.

The majority of mainstream criticism of cryptozoology is directed towards the search for megafauna cryptids such as Bigfoot, the Yeti, and the Loch Ness Monster which appear often in popular culture, but for which there is little or no scientific support. Scientists argue that mega-fauna cryptids are unlikely to exist undetected in great enough numbers to maintain a breeding population, and are unlikely to be able to survive in their reported habitats due to issues of climate and food supply.

As such, cryptozoology has never been embraced by the scientific community. Most experts on the matter consider the Bigfoot legend to be a combination of folklore and hoaxes, and cryptozoology is considered a pseudoscience by mainstream zoologists and biologists. Noted objections to cryptozoology include unreliable eyewitness accounts, lack of scientific and physical evidence, and over-reliance on confirmation (confirmation bias) rather than refutation.

Defenders

Supporters often argue that cryptozoological evidence is evaluated not on its merits or failings, but rather based on opinions of researchers, or on prevailing paradigms or world views. For example, biological anthropologists Grover Krantz and Jeff Meldrum have cited what they perceive to be ample physical evidence in support of the existence of Bigfoot, suggesting a surviving population of gigantopithecines. However, their arguments regarding Bigfoot have largely been dismissed by other scientists. Another supposedly well-attested cryptid that was largely ignored by scientists was the Minnesota Iceman of the 1960s, purportedly an unidentified hominid corpse inspected by two cryptozoologists, Ivan T. Sanderson and Bernard Heuvelmans.

Supporters claim that as in legitimate scientific fields, cryptozoologists are often responsible for disproving their own objects of study, for example, some cryptozoologists have collected evidence that disputes the validity of some facets of the Bigfoot phenomenon.

Cryptozoology supporters have claimed that in the early days of Western exploration of the world, many native tales of local animals initially dismissed as superstition by Western scientists were later proven to have a basis in biological fact, and that many unfamiliar animals, when initially reported, were considered hoaxes, delusions or misidentification.

There are several species cited as examples for continuing cryptozoological efforts. Cryptzoologists claim the Mountain gorilla (Gorilla gorilla) was previously dismissed as folklore/myth, due to lack of evidence and fossils, before being confirmed in 1902. The coelacanth, a "living fossil" which represents an order of fish believed to have been extinct for 65 million years, was identified from a specimen found in a fishing net in 1938 off the coast of South Africa. According to Dash, the Coelacanth is a good case for paying close attention to natives' knowledge of animals: though the fish's survival was a complete surprise to outsiders, it was so well known to locals that natives commonly used the fish's rough scales as a sort of sandpaper.

The 1976 discovery of the previously unknown megamouth shark off Oahu, Hawaii, has been cited by cryptozoologists to support the existence of other purported marine cryptids. Zoologist Ben S. Roesch agrees the discovery of megamouth proves "the oceans have a lot of secrets left to reveal," but simultaneously cautions against applying the "megamouth analogy" too broadly to hypothetical creatures, as the megamouth avoided discovery due to specific behavioral adaptations that would not fit most other cryptids. Cryptozoologists contend that as deep ocean remain unexplored, cryptozoological claims about oceanic cryptids should be given more credence. By plotting the discovery rate of new species, C. G. M. Paxton estimated that as many as 47 large oceanic species remain undiscovered. While the Megamouth is not a useful analogy to support the existence of marine "cryptids" in general, it does demonstrate the resistance of science to identify new large species of marine animals without a corpse. Sightings of Megamouths now number approximately one a year. Before the discovery, one could argue this consistent sighting record was also present, but that the sightings were ignored or discredited as of some other animal.

The Hoan Kiem Turtle was previously thought to be a local legend and classified as a cryptid, before conclusive evidence for its existence was accepted around 1998-2002. The 2003 discovery of the fossil remains of Homo floresiensis, thought to be a descendant of earlier Homo erectus, was cited by paleontologist Henry Gee of the journal Nature, as possible evidence that humanoid cryptids like the orang pendek and Yeti were "founded on grains of truth." Additionally, Gee declared, "cryptozoology, the study of such fabulous creatures, can come in from the cold."

Chapter 2: Bigfoot

Bigfoot is the name given to a large bipedal ape like creature reported to roam the remote forest areas of the United States, specifically the Pacific North West, California, the Rocky Mountains, the Great Lakes region, and some of the Northeast and Southern states. Bigfoot is most likely very closely related if not the same species as Canada's Sasquatch, similar reports of a creature like Bigfoot have been reported all over the world, including, Malaysia, China, Russia, Australia and South America to name a few.

Individuals who claim to have seen Bigfoot often give very similar descriptions, a 7 to 9 foot tall, ape or human like bipedal creature with broad shoulders, no visible neck, and pointed head similar to the crest of a male gorilla. Reports also sometimes note large eyes, a pronounced brow, and a large, low set forehead. A pungent odor, similar to feces, sewage or strong body odor, is also associated with most Bigfoot sightings.

As the name would suggest the creature also appears to have some very large feet. According to the late Smithsonian Primatologist John Napier noted that "the term Bigfoot has been in use since the early 1920's to describe large, unaccountable human like footprints in the Pacific Northwest," According to the renowned Cryptozoologist Loren Coleman the term Bigfoot was first used in print by Humboldt Times Columnist Andrew Genzoli on October 5, 1958 after construction worker Jerry Crew entered the Humboldt newsroom with plaster casts he made of gigantic footprints he discovered embedded in the mud near Bluff Creek Valley.

Ecologist Robert Pyle describes most Bigfoot tracks as commonly measuring fifteen to eighteen inches or more in length, having five toes, a double muscle ball, and a low arch. Some foot prints that come out of north Louisiana appear to only have 3 toes, some researchers into this phenomenon believe that the local Bigfoot population has been cut off from their major roots of travel and forced to inbreed. It is a known scientific fast that fingers and toes are one of the first things effected by inbreeding.

The earliest documented reports of a large ape like creature in the Pacific Northwest date back to 1924, after a series of alleged encounters at a gorge on the northeast shoulder of Mount St. Helens in Washington State. This gorge, which runs along the Plains of Abraham, narrows to as close as eight feet in some places and would later be named Ape Canyon due to the number of reports of ape like creatures in the area. Ape Canyon was reportedly the site of a violent encounter in 1924, between a group of minors and a group of Bigfoot. The minors account was published in several July 1924 issues of The Oregonian, a major daily newspaper in Portland Oregon. One of the Minors, Fred Beck, claimed that the minors shot and killed a large ape like creature and that night a group of Bigfoot attacked their cabin and tried to break in.

The director of the Western Speleological Survey, William Halliday, claimed in his 1983 pamphlet "Ape Cave and the Mount Saint Helens' Apes" that the minor's assailants where actually local youth. Until the very last summer of Ape Canyon existence in 1979, the canyon was almost completely destroyed by the 1980 eruption of Mount St. Helens, counselors from the YMCA's Camp Meehan on nearby Spirit Lake brought hikers to the canyons edge and retold a tradition that the 1924 incident was actually the result of young campers throwing light pumas stones into the canyon, not realizing there where minors at the bottom. Looking up the minors would have only seen dark moonlit figures throwing stones at their camp, the narrow walls of the canyon would have served to distort the voices of the YMCA campers enough to frighten the men below.

However, Halliday's explanation may fail to account for several factors:

• Beck claimed that the "apes" were seen clearly enough to note that they were not human;

• Beck claimed that one of the "apes" was shot and killed, but its unclear if Halliday claims that one of the stone-throwing teenagers was shot and killed in 1924.

• According to a series of 1924 articles in The Oregonian, multiple reporters and other eyewitnesses saw damage to the cabin, and enormous footprints at the scene, and it's difficult to imagine how stone throwing teenagers might have caused these details.

Another strange occurrence associated with the Ape Canyon area happened in 1950. A skier by the name of Jim Carter was with a group of men but went off by himself to film a documentary and was never seen again. During a massive search of the area to locate Jim one of the search team members said he had a chilling feeling of being watched the entire time. Carter's ski tracks seemed to indicate that he took off at a very high speed, making tremendous jumps that not even an experienced skier would attempt to make unless frightened beyond reason or being chased.

The majority of Bigfoot reports come from areas with very low human populations, however many do originate from parks located near major cities, cities like Portland, Oregon, Washington, DC, and Baltimore, Maryland to name a few. In addition most sightings occur near rivers, creeks, or lakes, and from areas where annual rain fall exceeds twenty inches. Researchers point out that these common factors indicate patterns of living species occupying an ecological niche, as opposed to hoaxed sightings.

Critics suggest people may have mistaken bears for Bigfoot, as sightings are some times near the known habitats of bears. However, witnesses include experienced hunters and outdoors men who claim to be familiar with bears and insist that the creatures they saw were not bears. Biologist John Bindernagel argues that there are marked differences between bears and Bigfoot sightings that make confusion unlikely. He noted that the profile of a bears snout is far different than that of a Bigfoot's flat face. In frontal view, Bigfoot's square broad shoulders contrast with that of a bears more tapered shoulders. Bigfoot also has relatively long legs that allow for a fluid and graceful stride, which is in large contract to the short legged shuffles of a bear when it walks on its hind legs. A bears ears are also naturally visible, while those of the Bigfoot are often hidden under long hair.

It has been suggested that a large number of people reporting Bigfoot sightings could be the victims of a hoax or possibly confused about what they actually encountered.. John Napier wrote that however accurate and sincere witness might seem, "eyewitness reports must be treated with considerable caution. Although we don't always know what we see, we tend to see what we know". He also adds, "without checking possible ulterior motivations, eyewitnesses cannot be acceptable as primary data".

Eyewitness reports will never be enough to make main stream science recognize the existence of Bigfoot, which is why Bigfoot researchers have made numerous claims that there is physical evidence to support the existence of Bigfoot. However the physical evidence which has been presented is seen minimal interest from the so called mainstream experts and is regarded as far from conclusive. This physical evidence takes many forms including footprints, hand prints, fingerprints, the Skookum body cast, hair samples and blood samples.

Although rare, Bigfoot's footprints seem to be the most common form of physical evidence that would suggest a large bipedal creature exists. Cryptozoologists often use plaster casts and photographs to document presumed Bigfoot footprints. Anthropologist Grover Krantz writes, "the push off mound in mid footprint is one of the most impressive pieces of evidence to me." The mound he refers to is a small grouping of soil created by a horizontal push of the forefoot just before it leaves the ground, which is present in some Bigfoot tracks. Krantz argues that neither artificial wood nor rubber Bigfoot feet could create this convincing feature, as he himself discovered after many attempts. Krantz also notes that reported Bigfoot steps are in excess of three feet, arguing that the enormous step would be difficult and almost impossible for any hoaxer to create.

Respected Bigfoot Researcher Loren Coleman and Jerome Clark, a well respected UFO researcher, write that there are some Bigfoot footprints that are hoaxes, but argue that they are often clumsy in comparison to presumably genuine footprints, which show distinctive forensic features that to an investigator would indicate that they are not fakes. Krantz also noted that toe positions can and do vary from one imprint to another on the same foot. It is Krantz's opinion that Bigfoot toes are more mobile than those on civilized human feet and that hoaxing this detail would require detailed knowledge of anatomy as well as dozens if not hundreds of different casts for each set of Bigfoot tracks, making a hoax very unlikely in these cases.

Researcher Henry Franzoni writes: "A strong piece of evidence which suggests that the footprints are not due to a hoax or hoaxers is from Dr. Henner Farenbach. He has studied a database of 550 track cast length measurements and has made some interesting observations. The Gaussian distribution of the 550 footprint lengths gives a curve that is very similar to the curve given by living populations of known animals with out much sexual dimorphism in footprint lengths. The standard error is very low, so additions to the database will not affect the result very much. It is not very likely that coordinated groups of hoaxers conspiring together for 38 years, the time span covered by the database of track measurements, could provide such a life like distribution in footprint lengths. Groups of hoaxers who did not conspire together would almost certainly result in a non Gaussian distribution for the database of footprint lengths."

In 1969 a series of alleged Bigfoot tracks where found near Bossburg, Washington, these footprints appeared to show that the creature's right foot was affected by Clubfoot, a birth defect which, if left untreated, will make the person affected appear to walk on their ankles, or on the sides of their feet. These deformed footprints are consistent with genuine disfigurement, and some argue that a hoax is unlikely. John Napier wrote, "It is very difficult to conceive of a hoaxer so subtle, so knowledgeable; and so sick; who would deliberately fake a footprint of this nature. I suppose it is possible, but it is so unlikely that I am prepared to discount it." Krantz declared that "analysis of the apparent anatomy of these tracks proved to be the first convincing evidence that the animals were real."

Another argument offered for the existence of Bigfoot are hand prints, Krantz cited two alleged Bigfoot hand prints from northern Washington State in the summer of 1970. He claims that the left handed prints showed a very broad, flat palm, more than twice as broad as his own, larger than average hands, with stubby fingers, lacking an opposable thumb. Krantz went on to write that the prints have many irregularities which cannot be identified in terms of human anatomy. Krantz obtained another pair of alleged hand prints from Paul Freeman, an American Bigfoot hunter in the late 1980's, he judged these prints as genuine as well for similar reasons as the first.

Several alleged hand and footprint impressions containing dermal ridges, fingerprints, have been discovered, this is significant because fingerprints are only present on humans and other primates, suggesting that they are not a hoax. Krantz reports that he offered casts of these prints to more than forty individual law enforcement fingerprint specialists across Canada and the United States for study. The reactions that he received ranged from "'very interesting' and 'they sure look real' to 'there is no doubt these are real.' The only exception was the Federal Bureau of Investigation expert who reportedly said something to the effect of 'The implications of this are just too much; I can't believe it's real'".

One of the casts with visible fingerprints showed what Krantz took to be sweat pores. Krantz reports that police expert Benny Kling commented that anyone who could engrave ridge detail of such quantity and quality should be making counterfeit money..This same print showed dysphasia, a common minor irregularity. Krantz writes, "The late Robert Olson was particularly impressed with this irregularity, as was Ed Palma of the San Diego Police Department".

Perhaps the most interested cast evidence of Bigfoot is the Skookum Body Cast. The Skookum Cast is a plaster cast taken on September 22, 2000 during a Bigfoot Field Researchers Organization expedition to the Skookum Meadows area of the Gifford Pinchot National Forest in Washington state. The cast, which measures 3 ½ by 5 feet and weighs approximately 400 lbs, is said to be of a partial body imprint in the mud. Some researchers believe the imprint was made by a living Bigfoot, which was evidently sitting on the ground to reach for fruit set out as bait by the researchers the previous night. Indeed, the body dimensions of the cast are reportedly 40 to 50 percent larger than that of a six-foot tall human and shows the imprint of a huge forearm, hip, thigh, heel ankle, and Achilles tendon. Impressions of hair are evident on the buttocks and thigh surfaces of the cast, as well as much longer fringes of hair on the forearm region. Dermal ridges appear on the heel, with many of the same characteristics consistently found on other purported Bigfoot samples.

Henner Fahrenbach, a biomedical scientist from Beaverton, Oregon, analyzed hair samples from the cast and identified a single distinctly primate hair, which he believes belongs to a Bigfoot. The heel, ankle and Achilles tendon impressions in the cast were studied by Jeff Meldrum of Idaho State University, and the anatomy is comparable to models of a Bigfoot foot Meldrum created after examining hundreds of alleged Sasquatch footprints. The cast has also been investigated by many leading Bigfoot researchers, including John Green, Grover Krantz, John Bindernagel, and Meldrum, who believe the cast to be authentic, and solid evidence of the existence of Bigfoot.

Plaster casts are not all that we have to show for our selves after years of collecting Bigfoot evidence, we have also managed to find several possible blood and hair samples over the years. In 1968 hairs retrieved from a bush in Riggins, Idaho were given to Roy Pinker, a police science instructor at California State University in Los Angeles. After studying the hairs Pinker was able to conclude that the hair samples did not match any samples from known animal species. Pinker also noted that he could not attribute them as being Bigfoot hairs with out an actual Bigfoot hair sample to compare it to. It is important to note that the analysis by Pinkered did not use DNA testing as it was not in use at the time.

Hair samples were also taken from a house located on the Lummi Indian reservation in Washington along with three more samples retrieved from Maryland, Oregon and California. Forensic Anthropologist Dr. Ellis R. Kerley and Physical Anthropologist Dr. Stephen Rosen of the University of Maryland, as well as Tom Moore, the Supervisor of the Wyoming Game and Fish Laboratory, examined the hair samples and stated that all the hair samples matched in terms of belonging to a "non species specific mammal". They concurred in finding that the four sets matched each other, were similar to gorilla and human but were neither, and they did not match 84 other species of North American mammals. Blood associated with the sample from Idaho was tested by Dr. Vincent Sarich of the University of California and found to be that of an unknown higher primate. These too were not subjected to DNA testing, which was not available at the time.

Several audio recordings that may suggest that Bigfoot is real have been brought to light, analysis of suspected Bigfoot vocalizations were analyzed by leading bioacoustics expert Dr. Robert Benson of Texas A&M University, Corpus Christi, he reported that some recordings "left him puzzled", and helped change his opinion from being a raving skeptic to being curiously receptive of Bigfoot.

Video footage of large bipedal hominid have also been collected as evidence, none more well known and more fiercely debated than the Patterson-Gimlin film. This 53 second long motion picture was shot on October 20th 1967 by Roger Patterson and Robert Gimlin who claimed the video to be a genuine recording of a Bigfoot. Some researchers declared the video a hoax almost immediately, stating that it showed nothing more than a man in an ape suit. But others, such as physical anthropologist Grover Krantz, are convinced that the film showed an actual undiscovered creature. Others, such as ecologist Robert Michael Pyle, refuse to state that the film is the real thing but admit that the video as never been adequately debunked.

Skeptics find it significant that the fossil record does not support the existence of Bigfoot and are quick to point out that other large North American animals like the cougar, moose, and mammoth are well represented. Yet, aside from clearly human remains, there is no evidence to suggest a prehistoric hominid or any other ape ever existed in North America. In addition no specimen of fossilized coprolite, dung, has ever been discovered, as is common with other ancient North American species.

Bigfoot researchers maintain that although there is an absence of fossil evidence dose not mean that there are no fossils of these creatures, just that they have not yet been discovered. Loren Coleman and Patrick Huyghe note that no one will look for such fossils if the creature involved is not thought to exist in the first place, and even with recognized primates fossil finds are normally meager at best. It is worth noting here that the majority of recognized primate species live in tropical rain forests where conditions are not ideal for creating fossils, in contrast there are thousands of known Native American mammal and human remains. Fossilization also requires ideal conditions, such as being covered by a landslide or mudslide shortly after death so that mineralization can take place on an undisturbed carcass.

Krantz suggests that the lack of Bigfoot remains alone is not a valid argument against the existence of the creature. He notes that most animals hide before dying and are then quickly lost to a number of different scavengers, he writes "I have yet to meet anyone who has found the remains of a bear that was not killed by human activity." It has also been suggested that if any Bigfoot remains were ever found, they may have been mistaken for larger than normal human remains. Unusually large American Indian remains, greater than 6 and a half feet tall, were often discovered in Ohio, Utah and Tennessee through out the 1800's. One such discover was documented by author John Haywood in his book, The Natural and Aboriginal History of Tennessee. In this book Haywood describes skeletons found in White County, Tennessee, in 1821 which averaged an estimated 7 feet in length. These findings left some researchers to wonder if perhaps the remains of a Bigfoot or many Bigfoot have in fact been discovered only to be mistaken for the remains of a taller than average human, if this was the case perhaps Bigfoot is far more human like than we originally thought.

The biggest problem with proving the existence of Bigfoot is not the lack of solid evidence but rather the abundance of hoaxed evidence. Perhaps the biggest claim of a hoax, besides that of the Patterson-Gimlin film was made in 2002 by the family of Raymond L. Wallace. After Mr. Wallace passed away, his family published what they claimed to be the details of many of Mr. Wallace Bigfoot hoaxes dating back to 1958. They even claimed that the footprint found by Jerry Crew at an isolated construction site in Humboldt County California, the very one that gave rise to the term Bigfoot, was the work of Mr. Wallace.

Giving some credibility to these claims was the fact that Raymond Wallace's brother, Wilbur L. Wallace was the over seer of the construction site Mr. Crew found the print at. However these claims and Mr. Wallace himself are poorly regarded by many who take the subject of Bigfoot seriously. Bigfoot supporters deny the family's claims and one writer even pointed out that the wooden track stompers shown to the media by the Wallace family do not match photos of the 1958 tracks they claim their father made, he continues by pointing out that the feet are a different shape all together.

Primatologist John Napier acknowledged that there have been some hoaxes but also stated that hoaxing is often an inadequate explanation for all of the Bigfoot sightings and tracks. Krantz later added that it would require something like 100,000 casual hoaxers to explain the many Bigfoot footprints.

The idea of Bigfoot is so clouded with dubious claims and hoaxes that many scientists do not give the subject the time of day. Napier wrote that the mainstream scientific community's indifference stems primarily from insufficient evidence. He also notes that scientists prefer to investigate the probable rather than beat their heads against the wall of the faintly possible. Krantz later stated that the scientific establishment generally resists new ideas, and there is good reason for it. Simply put, new and innovative ideas in science are almost always wrong.

Although most scientists find the current evidence in the case of Bigfoot unpersuasive, a number of respected experts have spoken out on the topic of Bigfoot. In an interview on National Public Radio in 2002, Jane Goodall publicly expressed her belief in Bigfoot, saying, "Well, I'm a romantic, so I always wanted them to exist. Of course the big criticism of all this is, where is the body? You know, why isn't there a body? I can't answer that, and maybe they don't exist, but I want them to."

In 2004, Henry Gee, editor of the prestigious Nature, argued that creatures like Bigfoot deserved further study, writing, "The discovery that Homo floresiensis survived until so very recently, in geological terms, makes it more likely that stories of other mythical, human-like creatures such as Yetis are founded on grains of truth . Now, cryptozoology, the study of such fabulous creatures, can come in from the cold."

In an essay entitled, Sasquatch Must Exist, published after his death, prominent anthropologist Carleton S. Coon wrote "Even before I read John Green's book, Sasquatch: The Apes Among Us, first published in 1973, I accepted Sasquatch's existence." Coon examines the question from several angles, stating that he is confident only in ruling out a relict Neanderthal population as a viable candidate for Sasquatch reports. Coon may have ruled out Neanderthal man as the identify of Bigfoot but many researchers point out other creatures which may possibly be behind Bigfoot sightings.

A large number of researchers, including Grover Krantz, feel that the most likely candidate to explain Bigfoot is a relict population of Gigantopithecus blacki, a very large ape known only by a few jaw bones and teeth fragments found in Southeast Asia. Fossils of Gigantopithecus have also been found in extreme eastern Siberia, which has forests similar to Northwestern North America. Believers in this theory suggest that like so many other recognized species, Gigantopithecus may have migrated across the Bering Strait, settling down in the forests of North America. This theory however is considered highly speculative, mainstream science views Gigantopithecus as a quadruped, and study of the Patterson-Gimlin film show a slender lower mandible, which does not match the massive lower jaw of Gigantopithecus. Assuming the Patterson-Gimlin footage is legitimate, Bigfoot and Gigantopithecus could not be one in the same.

John Napier and anthropologist Gordon Strasenburg believe that should a creature like Bigfoot exist the most likely candidate would be a species of Paranthropus, an extinct human genus which is thought to have inhabited forested areas of Africa some 2 million years ago. One member of this genus, scientific name Paranthropus robustus, would have looked very similar to Bigfoot, including the crested skull and naturally bipedal gait.

The American Indians believed that Bigfoot, although being a very real being, exists on a separate plane of existence than humans. According to the Indian's legend, Bigfoot is a spiritual being with the ability to cross between these planes of existence at will. Modern believers in the Indian legends will often site this ability to cross between planes as a means to explain why a Bigfoot corpse has never been found, also these believers feel that this would also explain why a breading population of Bigfoot has never been discovered.

There is also a little known subspecies of Homo erectus known as Meganthropus, which reportedly grew to enormous proportions. Some of the more extreme claims state that this giant could grow to heights greater than 9 feet tall and weighted up to 1000 pounds. Though a small handful of researchers believe that Meganthropus could be the true identity of Bigfoot, it is important to note that no official dimensions of this creature have been established and some evidence does suggest that it was no bigger than the average Homo erectus, also all known fossil evidence of Meganthropus was discovered thousands of miles away from North America on the Indonesian islands.

Although it is unclear what Bigfoot really is or if the creature even exists at all, enough evidence has been collected to warrant many formal studies of the creature. In 1955 Bernard Heuvelmans, who many consider to be the father of modern cryptozoology, discussed the existence of the Yeti in his book, On the Track of Unknown Animals.

In the 1960's Ivan T Sanderson wrote several articles on mysterious animals, including Bigfoot, some of which appeared in the Saturday Evening Post, a popular weekly magazine. Sanderson's book, Abominable Snowmen: Legend Comes to Life, is considered the first book length study of "hairy hominids" and certainly helped popularize the Bigfoot legend.

In the 1970's John Napier published what is considered to be the first mainstream scientific study of available evidence in his book, Bigfoot: The Yeti and Sasquatch in Myth and Reality. In 1974 The National Wildlife Federation funded a field study geared towards seeking out Bigfoot and related evidence, no notable discoveries were obtained from this study. In 1975, the existence of Bigfoot was briefly discussed in the book, The Gentle Giants: The Gorilla Story, co authored by noted anthropologist Geoffery H. Bourne. In May of 1978 the University of British Columbia hosted a symposium entitled, Anthropology of the Unknown: Sasquatch and Similar Phenomena, a Conference on Humanoid Monsters. All who attended, mostly people with a background in anthropology, took the topic seriously, and while few accepted the existence of such creatures, they jointly concluded that there is no ground to dismiss all the evidence as a hoax or misinterpretation.

After the 1970's boon in popularity there was only a hand full of formal academic scientific studies into Bigfoot.. In 1980 Marjorie Halpin and Michael Ames, using papers taken from the 1978 University of British Columbia symposium, published the book, Manlike Monsters on Trail: Early Records and Modern Evidence. In 2001 Reinhold Messner, an Italian Mountaineer, published the book, My Quest for the

Yeti: Confronting the Himalayas' Deepest Mystery, based on his1997 encounter with a Yeti. In his book Messner argues that the Yeti is actually an endangered Himalayan Brown Bear that has the ability to walk upright.

In addition to academic studies of Bigfoot several organizations have also been created which devote there time and resources to the study and exploration into the Bigfoot phenomena, the most well known of these organizations is the Bigfoot Field Researchers Organization. The BFRO was founded in 1995 and seeks to resolve the mystery surrounding the legend of Bigfoot, the main goal of the BFRO is to derive conclusive documentation of the species' existence. According to the BFRO website this goal is pursued through the proactive collection of empirical data and physical evidence from the field and by means of activities designed to promote an awareness and understanding of the nature and origin of the evidence.

The BFRO, the oldest and largest organization of its kind, is directed by a virtual community of scientists, journalists, and specialists from diverse backgrounds. The researchers who compose the BFRO are constantly engaged in projects including field and laboratory investigations designed to address various aspects of the Bigfoot phenomenon. As a result of the education and experience of its members and the quality of their efforts, the BFRO is widely considered as the most credible and respected investigative network involved in the study of this subject.

In recent years, thanks to the efforts of these organizations and individuals like Loren Coleman, Bigfoot's popularity has reached record levels. Main steam television stations have cashed in on the popularity of Bigfoot and produced a multitude of shows and movies on the creature. The Sci Fi Channel has produced several original movies on the creature and the National Geographic Channel featured Bigfoot as the topic of one of its hour long broadcasts of "Is It Real?" The Discovery and History Channels have also featured Bigfoot in several of their shows geared towards the unknown. Resent advertising has also helped to push Bigfoot into mainstream pop culture, an example of this would be the "Messin With Sasquatch" commercials by Jack Links Beef Jerky, which show a couple of hikers who stumble upon a Bigfoot doing day to day things like sleeping or cooking and decide to play a prank on the creature such as putting shaving cream in his hand then tickling his nose, we all know that classic prank, or unscrewing the top of his salt shaker so that when he goes to use it the salt spills all over his food.

Bigfoot has also appeared in text at an increasing rate over the last few years, appearing in everything from supermarket tabloids to more serious writings. For example, The Weekly World News occasionally runs stories on the creature, and several novels have been written based on Bigfoot, such as the book Monster, which describes the kidnapping of a woman by a group of Bigfoot. Bigfoot has even appeared as a character in several Marvel Comics, this mutant, named Sasquatch, could transform from an ordinary looking human into a creature resembling the legendary Bigfoot. Toronto based, Graham Roumieu, wrote and illustrated two comical books about Bigfoot, The first titled, Me Write Book: It Bigfoot Memoir, and the second titled, In Me Own Words: The Autobiography of Bigfoot.

With new sightings of Bigfoot being reported everyday and more plaster casts of the creature's foot than we know what to do with, at the end of the day we are still no closer to proving the existence of Bigfoot than we were the days past. Could the whole thing be, as some suggest, a mass case of War of the Worlds syndrome, people seeing things that aren't really there just because they are told that something is there? And until a body or live creature is brought back to be examined by science the truth is we may never be able to fully explain the Bigfoot phenomena The burden of proof now rests on the shoulders of believers, science tells us Bigfoot does not exist, its up to us to tell science otherwise. And thus we leave you with the words of John Napier, "If one track and one report are true bill, then myth must be chucked out the window and reality admitted through the front door."

The Evidence

Physical evidence to support the existence of Bigfoot comes in many forms, the following is a brief overview of the different types of evidence which has been presented to the scientific community.

Footprints – Though rare themselves, plaster casts and photos of alleged Bigfoot footprints are the most common form of physical evidence discovered to date. Often dismissed as hoaxes by main stream science, some of these casts display features which, according to many experts, could not have been faked. Features including push off mounds, varying toe positions and one case of club foot are considered to specific to be the work of a hoaxer using plastic or wooden feet.

Hand prints – A few reports of Bigfoot hand prints have been studied over the years. These so called hand prints are generally flat palmed and more than twice the size of a normal humans hand.

Dermal Ridges – Also known as fingerprints these dermal ridges have been discovered on several foot and hand print molds. These casts have been studied by top police fingerprint experts and found to be to difficult to hoax, including some that appear to have been damaged, such as a cut or gash in the skin, and then healed over creating distinct patterns. If these where to be hoaxed it would take a person with intimate knowledge of biology and healing of the skin. Its important to note that prints with dermal ridges so important because dermal ridges themselves are only found on humans and primates.

Skookum Body Cast -.The Skookum Cast is a plaster cast taken on September 22, 2000 during a Bigfoot Field Researchers Organization expedition to the Skookum Meadows area of the Gifford Pinchot National Forest in Washington state. The cast, which measures 3 ½ by 5 feet and weighs approximately 400 lbs, is said to be of a partial body imprint in the mud. Some researchers believe the imprint was made by a living Bigfoot, which was evidently sitting on the ground to reach for fruit set out as bait by the researchers the previous night.

Hair Samples – Several hair samples believed to be from Bigfoot have been collected and studied over the years. Normally these hairs turn out to belong to common animals such as deer or bears, however on rare occasions a hair will prove to belong to an unknown primate species. With out an actual Bigfoot hair to compare these hairs to it is impossible to say for sure that that they come from the legendary creature, but that fact that someone has found an unknown primate hair in the United States is reason to consider the possibility.

The Sightings

There are so many sightings of Bigfoot that we could not possibly list them all here, however below you will find several of the more significant sightings through out the years.

1840: Protestant missionary Reverend Elkanah Walker records myths of hairy giants persistent among Native Americans living in Spokane, Washington. The Indians report that said giants steal salmon and have a strong smell.

1893: An account by Theodore Roosevelt is published this year in The Wilderness Hunter. Roosevelt relates a story which was told to him by "a beaten old mountain hunter, named Bauman" living in Idaho. Some have suggested similarities to Bigfoot reports.

In July 1924, Fred Beck and four other miners claim to have been attacked by several Bigfoot in Ape Canyon. The creatures reportedly hurl large rocks at the miners' cabin for several hours during the night. This case was publicized in newspaper reports printed in 1924.

1940s Onward: People living in Fouke, Arkansas report that a Bigfoot like creature, dubbed the "Fouke Monster", inhabits the region. A high number of reports occur in the Boggy Creek area and are the basis for the 1973 film The Legend of Boggy Creek.

1958: Two construction workers, Leslie Breazale and Ray Kerr, report seeing a Bigfoot about 45 miles northeast of Eureka, California. 16 inch tracks had previously been spotted in the Northern California woods.

On October 20, 1967, Roger Patterson and Robert Gimlin capture a purported Bigfoot on film in Bluff Creek, California.

On August 28, 1995, a TV film crew from Waterland Productions pull off the road into Jedediah Smith Redwoods State Park, and film what they claim to be a sasquatch in their RV's Headlights.

On May 30th 1996, Loni and Owen where on a fishing trip with family and friends at Chopaka Lake in Washington State, when they spotted something in a near by field. The resulting video footage appears to show a Bigfoot running full spread across the field.

The Stats

• Classification: Hominid

• Size: 6 – 9 feet tall

• Weight: 400 plus pounds

• Diet: Reports vary, some suggest vegetarian others place deer in the Bigfoot's Diet

• Location: All over the United States, mainly in the Pacific North West and Texas

• Movement: Upright Bipedal Walking

• Environment: Remote Forests, though some suggest that migratory paths may take the Bigfoot through more populated areas.

Chapter 3: Mothman

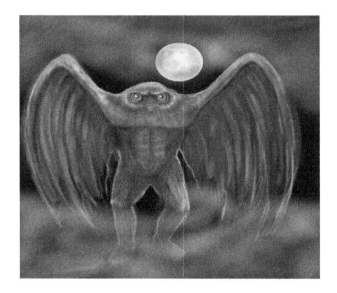

The Mothman, a strange creature reported to haunt the Charleston and Point Pleasant areas of West Virginia between November 1966 and December 1967, was also sporadically reported to be seen prior to, and after, those dates, with some sightings coming as recently as 2005. Most observers describe the Mothman as being 5 to 7 feet tall creature with wings and large reflective red eyes, similar to the Garuda of Hindu lore. A number of hypotheses have been put forward to explain what people reported, ranging from misidentification and coincidence to paranormal phenomena and conspiracy theories.

The Mothman was named in parallel to the villain "Killer Moth" in the Batman TV series that was popular at the time, was reportedly first sighted November 12, 1966. A group of five men were preparing a grave in a cemetery close to Clendenin, West Virginia when what they described as a "brown human shape with wings" lifted off from behind nearby trees and flew over their heads. However, this sighting was not made public until later, and the first sighting described in the media took place just three days later.

On the evening of November 15, 1966 two young married couples from Point Pleasant, Roger and Linda Scarberry and Steve and Mary Mallette, were out for a drive in the Scarberrys' car. They were passing a World War II TNT factory about seven miles outside of Point Pleasant, in the 2,500 acre McClintic Wildlife Station, when they noticed two red lights in the shadow by an old generator plant near the gate of the factory. They stopped the car and were startled to see that the lights were the glowing red eyes of a large animal, "shaped like a man, but bigger, maybe six and a half or seven feet tall, with big wings folded against its back," according to Roger Scarberry. Terrified, the couples took off in their car, heading for Route 62.

Headed down the exit ramp, they saw the creature again, standing on a ridge near the road. It spread its wings and took off, following their car to the city limits. They went to the Mason County courthouse and told their story to Deputy Millard Halstead, who later said "I've known these kids all their lives. They'd never been in any trouble and they were really scared that night. I took them seriously." He followed Roger Scarberry's car back to the TNT factory, but found no sign of the strange creature. According to the book Alien Animals, by Janet Board, a poltergeist attack on the Scarberry home took place later that night, in which the creature was seen several times.

On that very same evening, at about 10:30 pm Newell Partridge, a local building contractor who lived in Salem, about 90 miles from point pleasant, was watching television when he the screen suddenly went dark. He would later state that a weird pattern filled the screen and that he heard a loud whining sound coming from outside that raised in pitch before drawing silent, "It sounded like a generator winding up". Newell's dog, Bandit, began to stir and howl out of the front porch, Newell got up to investigate what was going on. When he walked outside, he noticed that Bandit was focused on the hay barn, about 150 yards from the house. Newell then turned on his flashlight and shinned the beam in the direction of the barn, upon doing so the light illuminated two red circles that looked like eyes or the reflectors of a bicycle tire, the sight of these glowing red eyes frightened him. Bandit, an experienced hunting dog who was also very protective of his territory shot off across the yard in the direction of the glowing eyes. Newell called for his dog to stop and come back to the porch but the determined dog paid no attention to his master.

Afraid for the life of his dog Newell ran back into the house to get his gun but was to frightened to go back outside. That night he slept with with his gun propped up against his bed. The next morning Bandit was no where to be found, Newell called out for his dog but to no avail. Two days later there was still no sign of Bandit when Newell read about the Mothman sightings in Point Pleasant. He read one statement in particular that may have explained the fate of his beloved dog. Roger Scarberry, one of the 4 people who originally saw the Mothman near the old TNT plant, was quoted by the newspaper as saying that they saw the body of a large dog laying on the side of the road moments before the Mothman appeared to them. Could this have been to body of Bandit?

The next night, November 16, local townspeople, armed, went searching the area around the old TNT plant for signs of Mothman. This old World War II TNT plant would become known as the lair of the Mothman, and the strange creature could not have picked a better place to hide. The area was made up of several hundred acres of woods and large concrete domes where explosives where stored during the war. A network of tunnels branched out across the area and made it possible for the creature to move about without being noticed. The area was also surrounded by the McClintic Wildlife Station, a heavily forested animal preserve filled with dense woods, artificial and natural ponds, and steep ridges and hills. Much of the reserve was inaccessible by vehicle and any creature, including the Mothman, could have remained hidden.

Mr. and Mrs. Raymond Wamsley and Mrs. Marcella Bennett with her baby daughter Teena, were in a car on their way to visit their friends, Mr. and Mrs. Ralph Thomas, who lived in a bungalow among the igloos which where concrete dome shaped structures erected for explosives storage during WWII close to the TNT plant. The igloos were now empty, some owned by the county, some by companies intending to use them for storage. They were headed back to their car when a figure appeared behind the parked vehicle. Mrs. Bennett said it seemed like it had been lying down, slowly rising up from the ground, large and gray, with glowing red eyes. Mrs. Bennett reportedly was so terrified that she dropped her young daughter but quickly got her thoughts together, picked up her child and ran back into the house. Wamsley phoned the police as the terrified friends heard the creature walk onto the porch and peering in through the windows. By the time the police got to the house the creature had disappeared.

On November 24, four people saw the Mothman flying through the air over the TNT area. On the morning of November 25, Thomas Ury, who was driving along Route 62 north of the TNT, said he saw the creature standing in a field by the road, then spread its wings and took off, following his car as he sped into Point Pleasant to report the sighting to the sheriff.

On November 26, Mrs. Ruth Foster of Charleston, West Virginia saw the Mothman standing on her front lawn, but it was gone when her brother-in-law went out to look. On the morning of November 27, it pursued a young woman near Mason, West Virginia, and was reported again in St. Albans the same night, by two children. The Mothman was seen again January 11, 1967, and several times during 1967. Fewer sightings of the Mothman were reported after the collapse of the Silver Bridge, when 46 people died. The Silver Bridge, so named for its aluminum paint, was an eyebar chain suspension bridge that connected the cities of Point Pleasant, West Virginia and Gallipolis, Ohio over the Ohio River.

It was built in 1928 and collapsed on December 15, 1967; investigation of the wreckage pointed to the failure of a single eye-bar in a suspension chain due to a small flaw when it was made. Some researchers believe that the appearance of the Mothman brings about a warning of tragedy to come, and say that the sightings of the Mothman in Point Pleasant was due to the imminent collapse of the ill fated bridge.

Reports of Mothman sightings and events continue to this day. Instances of "strange flying creatures" and "winged men" have been reported in many American states as well as across the globe in Europe, Asia and the Middle East, including supposed sightings in Chernobyl, Ukraine in 1986, shortly before the Chernobyl Nuclear Disaster.

A large collection of first-hand material about Mothman is found in John Keel's 1975 book The Mothman Prophecies, in which Keel lays out the chronology of Mothman and what he claims to be related parapsychological events in the area, including UFO activity, Men in Black encounters, poltergeist activity, Bigfoot and black panther sightings, animal and human mutilations, precognitions by witnesses, and the December 15, 1967 collapse of the Silver Bridge across the Ohio River. Keel's first book was the basis of a 2002 movie of the The Mothman Prophecies, starring Richard Gere, Laura Linney and Debra Messing, directed by Mark Pellington. A companion book called The Eighth Tower was also released in 1975, built on material edited from The Mothman Prophecies by the publishers.

John Keel believes that Point Pleasant was a "window" area, a place that was marked by long periods of strange sightings, monster reports and the coming and going of unusual persons. He states that it may be wrong to blame the collapse of the bridge on the local UFO sightings, but the intense activity in the area at the time does suggest some sort of connection. Others have pointed to another supernatural link to the strange happenings, blaming the events on the legendary Cornstalk Curse that was placed on Point Pleasant in the 1770's.

Author Jeff Wamsley has compiled two books on the Point Pleasant Mothman phenomenon. In his 2002 book Mothman: The Facts Behind the Legend, with Donnie Sergent, Jr., Wamsley presents old press clippings, local history, and eyewitness interviews. In his second book, Mothman: Behind the Red Eyes written in 2005, Wamsley interviews nearly a dozen eyewitnesses, allowing them to describe what they saw. Wamsley is also the owner of the Mothman Museum and a key organizing figure in the Mothman Festival each year in Point Pleasant, West Virginia.

A.B. Colvin, a local photojournalist and documentary film maker who claims to have seen the creature in 1967 and 1973, has produced a book and 32-hour DVD news series on Mothman called The Mothman's Photographer, with over 40 eyewitnesses and experts. Colvin's sister took a snapshot of him in 1973 that allegedly shows a Garuda or Thunderbird in the background. Colvin took a picture of an anomalous figure in a crop circle in 1979 that he alleges could be either his deceased father, who Colvin reports was at the supposed Philadelphia Experiment in 1943, or Indrid Cold, a 'spaceman' who reportedly contacted local resident Woody Derenberger.

While researching various forms of Buddhist philosophy and various Native tribes, Colvin seems to have reached the conclusion that both the Garuda of the Far East and the Thunderbird of the Native Americans are synonymous with Mothman, and that the Mothman was fulfilling a pre-ordained, archetypal role that involves stopping heinous crimes at pivotal moments in mankind's cyclical existence by sending visions, dreams, and messages to ordinary humans. Colvin presents some evidence that Charleston witnesses separately saw Mothman, the Dover Demon, the Virgin Mary, plasma figures, "intelligent" globes of light, and the Flatwoods monster in the same spot, lending credence to his Mothman "shape-shifting" theory.

Cryptozoologist and author Loren Coleman, in the 2002 book Mothman and Other Curious Encounters focuses on news stories he alleges undermine Keel's "ultra terrestrial" approach. As Coleman likes to point out, the word "Mothman" was coined by a copy editor in Ohio who was a fan of the television "Batman" series. Coleman alleges that the Indrid Cold story told by Woodrow Derenberger has little or nothing to do with the core Mothman reports. He claims that over eighty people have died because they have seen, researched, or had some connection to Mothman, such as the wife of the director of the 2002 motion picture, who also worked on a Mothman film. Coleman feels that the influence of Keel has heightened the cryptozoological realities that underlie the initial reports. He claims he does not consider mundane natural history explanations as the final answer.

Skeptics such as a college professor in 1966 and members of CSICOP in 2002 have argued that the most likely explanation of the sightings is excited eyewitnesses mistaking a barn owl for a winged monster. Another possibility is the misidentification of a sandhill crane. The sandhill crane, however, is not native to the area but may have migrated down from Canada. This theory does not appease those who have witnessed the Mothman in person, stating that in no way could what they have seen actually have been a bird of any kind.

Omen of horrific events to come, demon, escaped government experiment, barn owl, Sandhill Crane or something else, what could the Mothman be? Unlike a lot of cryptids that are localized in a general area, the Mothman does not seem to appear in any one area for a long period of time making field research of the creature next to impossible. And if the theory that the Mothman is an omen of ill fortune would any field research even want to go looking for such a creature? The Mothman is one cryptid that will most likely remain a mystery for all time, flying eerily through the darkest places in our world and our subconscious

The Evidence

There is no physical evidence that would suggest that the creature known as the Mothman actually exists, no footprints, no fuzzy pictures, no hair samples or questionable video. Eyewitness reports are the only evidence we have to even suggest that this creature may actually exist, and as we all know, in the scientific community eye witness reports are worth about as much as that picture you took of Bigfoot, you know that one where your thumb covered up the lens.

The Sightings

• November 12, 1966 a group of five men were preparing a grave in a cemetery close to Clendenin, West Virginia when what they described as a "brown human shape with wings" lifted off from behind nearby trees and flew over their heads.

• On November 15, 1966 two young married couples from Point Pleasant, Roger and Linda Scarberry and Steve and Mary Mallette, were out for a drive in the Scarberrys' car. They were passing a World War II

TNT factory about seven miles outside of Point Pleasant, in the 2,500 acre McClintic Wildlife Station, when they noticed two red lights in the shadow by an old generator plant near the gate of the factory. They stopped the car and were startled to see that the lights were the glowing red eyes of a large animal, "shaped like a man, but bigger, maybe six and a half or seven feet tall, with big wings folded against its back," according to Roger Scarberry.

• On November 15th, 1966 at 10:30 pm Newell Partridge, a local building contractor who lived in Salem, about 90 miles from point pleasant, was watching television when he the screen suddenly went dark. He would later state that a weird pattern filled the screen and that he heard a loud whining sound coming from outside that raised in pitch before drawing silent, "It sounded like a generator winding up". Newell's dog, Bandit, began to stir and howl out of the front porch, Newell got up to investigate what was going on. When he walked outside, he noticed that Bandit was focused on the hay barn, about 150 yards from the house. Newell then turned on his flashlight and shinned the beam in the direction of the barn, upon doing so the light illuminated two red circles that looked like eyes or the reflectors of a bicycle tire.

• Mr. and Mrs. Raymond Wamsley and Mrs. Marcella Bennett with her baby daughter Teena, were in a car on their way to visit their friends, Mr. and Mrs. Ralph Thomas, who lived in a bungalow among the igloos which where concrete dome shaped structures erected for explosives storage during WWII close to the TNT plant. The igloos were now empty, some owned by the county, some by companies intending to use them for storage. They were headed back to their car when a figure appeared behind the parked vehicle. Mrs. Bennett said it seemed like it had been lying down, slowly rising up from the ground, large and gray, with glowing red eyes. Mrs. Bennett reportedly was so terrified that she dropped her young daughter but quickly got her thoughts together, picked up her child and ran back into the house. Wamsley phoned the police as the terrified friends heard the creature walk onto the porch and peering in through the windows. By the time the police got to the house the creature had disappeared.

• On November 24, four people saw the Mothman flying through the air over the TNT area.

• On the morning of November 25, Thomas Ury, who was driving along Route 62 north of the TNT, said he saw the creature standing in a field by the road, then spread its wings and took off, following his car as he sped into Point Pleasant to report the sighting to the sheriff.

• On November 26, Mrs. Ruth Foster of Charleston, West Virginia saw the Mothman standing on her front lawn, but it was gone when her brother-in-law went out to look.

• On the morning of November 27, the Mothman reportedly pursued a young woman near Mason, West Virginia, and was reported again in St. Albans the same night, by two children.

• In 1986, shortly before the Chernobyl Nuclear Disaster in Chernobyl, Ukraine the Mothman was supposedly sighed, giving some credibility to the idea that the creature is sign of a nearing horrific event.

The Stats

• Classification: Hybrid

- Size: Between 6 and 7 Feet Tall

- Weight: Unknown

- Diet: Unknown, Presumed Carnivorous

- Location: In and Around Point Pleasant, Scattered Reports World Wide

- Movement: Walking and Flight

- Environment: Unknown

Chapter 4: Jersey Devil

The Jersey Devil, a creature reported to dwell in the vast New Jersey Pinelands, is said to have haunted the area for over 260 years. The creature has been reported by over 2,000 eyewitnesses and been blamed for closing of schools and factories when sightings of the Jersey Devil where at their peak. The origins of The Jersey Devil are as mysterious as the creature its self, there are plenty of theories and legends of its birth but no one really knows for sure. One of the most popular legends states that a Mrs. Shrouds of Leeds Point, New Jersey, after finding out she was pregnant again, exclaimed that she wished this child would be the devil. The child was born misshapen and deformed, it was hidden from the public by the ashamed mother, however on the first stormy night the child began to flap his arms, all of a sudden the child's arms turned into wings and it flew out of the house through the chimney never to be seen by the family again.

Other local legends of the Jersey Devil include a story of a young girl who fell in love with a British soldier during the Revolutionary War, the people of leads point cursed the girl, when she gave birth the child was said to be the devil. Some others believe that the birth of the Jersey Devil was punishment from God for the mistreatment of a local minister by the people of Leeds point. Another, more popular, legend places the birth place of the Jersey Devil in Estelville, NJ. A Mrs. Leeds, after finding out she was pregnant with her 13th child, shouted, "I hope it's the devil." The child was born with horns, a tail, wings and a horse like head; it flew out the door upon birth. The creature visited Mrs. Leeds on a daily basis and every day Mrs. Leeds would tell it to go away, one day the creature stopped showing up. Yet another legend stats that in 1735, in Burlington, NJ the same Mrs. Leeds went into labor on a stormy night. The legend goes on to tell that Mrs. Leeds herself was a witch and the father of the child was the devil himself. The child was reportedly born normal, however shortly after birth transformed into a creature with hooves, a horse like head, bat like wings and a forked tail. The newly born devil proceeded to attack everyone in the room then flew up the chimney, circled the village and then headed off in the direction of the Pine Barrens. In 1740 a priest was brought in to exercise the devil from the area for 100 years, the creature was not seen again until 1890.

As different as all these legends may be, there are several similarities which tie the stories together. All the legends seem to agree that the name Leeds was part of the birth of the Jersey Devil, be it the mothers name or the birth place, most of the legends include the name. Alfred Heston, the historian for Atlantic County New Jersey, believes that the Jersey Devil could have been born to either the Leeds or the Shrouds families. Mr. Heston discovered that a Daniel Leeds opened land in Great Egg Harbor, NJ in 1699 and that the family home was located in Leeds Point. Mr. Heston also discovered that a Samuel Shrouds Sr. moved to Little Egg Harbor, NJ in 1735 and lived right across the river from the Leeds family house. Another interesting bit of information ties the Burlington legend in with the other legends. Professor Fred MacFadden of Coppin State College, Baltimore, discovered the mentioning of a Devil in writings from the Burlington area as early as 1735. Professor MacFadden also noted that back in the 1700's the name Burlington was used to describe the area from the city of Burlington to the Atlantic Ocean, this would mean that Leeds Point and Esterville, the other reported birthplaces of the Jersey Devil could have been referred to as the same place indicated in the Burlington Legend.

The Jersey Devil is not limited to just legends of the creature however; sightings of the beast have been reported in the Pine Barrens and surrounding areas since the early 19th Century. There are few documented sightings which still exist from before 1909; however the ones that did survive are quite compelling. In the early 19th century, Commodore Stephen Decatur, a navel war hero, was testing cannon balls on a firing range when he saw a strange creature flying across the sky. Joseph Bonaparte, former king of Spain and Brother of the famous Napoleon Bonaparte, reported seeing the Jersey Devil in Bordentown, NJ between 1816 and 1839 while out hunting. In the mid 1840's a strange creature with a piercing scream and odd hoof like foot prints began to kill live stock in the area around the Pine Barrens. Between 1859 and 1894, the Jersey Devil was sighted numerous times and reportedly carried off a large number of livestock and other small animals in Haddonfield, Bridgeton, Smithville, Long Branch, Brigantine and Leeds Point. The last reported sighting before the turn of the century was reported by George Saarosy, a prominent business man, while traveling the New York New Jersey Border.

In 1903, Charles Skinner, author of American Myths and Legends, claimed that the legend of the Jersey Devil had run its course and that New Jersey would no longer need to worry about it. The people of New Jersey went undisturbed by the creature for nearly 6 years, that is until the week of January 16th 1909. During this week the Jersey Devil would leave its tracks all over South Jersey and into Philadelphia, it was seen by well over 1,000 people.

It started on a Sunday morning, January 16th 1909 when Thack Cozzens of Woodbury, NJ, reported seeing a flying creature with glowing eyes flying down the street. In Bristol, PA, John Mcowen heard and saw the creature on the banks of a channel. Patrol James Sackville fired on the creature as it flew away screaming. E.W. Minister, Postmaster for Bristol also reported seeing a bird like creature with a horse head, he reported that the creature also had a piercing scream.

On Monday Morning the residents of Bristol found strange hoof prints in the snow, two local trappers examined the prints and claimed that they had never seen prints like them before. The Lowdens of Burlington, NJ, found hoof prints in their yard and around their trash, which was partially eaten. Almost every yard in Burlington had sets of strange footprints in them. The prints where up trees, went from roof to roof, disappeared in the middle of the road and stopped in the middle of open fields. The same tracks were also found in Columbus, Hedding, Kinhora and Rancocas. A hunt was organized to the follow the tracks but the dogs refused to follow the trail.

On Tuesday the 18th one of the longest sightings of the Jersey Devil was reported by a Mr. and Mrs. Nelson Evans of Gloucester when they were awakened by a strange noise. Upon looking out the winder Mr. Nelson witnessed what he claimed to be the Jersey Devil for 10 minutes. Mr. Evans went on to describe the creature he saw that day:" It was about three feet and half high, with a head like a collie dog and a face like a horse. It had a long neck, wings about two feet long, and its back legs were like those of a crane, and it had horse's hooves. It walked on its back legs and held up two short front legs with paws on them. It didn't use the front legs at all while we were watching. My wife and I were scared, I tell you, but I managed to open the window and say, 'Shoo', and it turned around barked at me, and flew away." Shortly after that sighting, two professional hunters tracked the Jersey Devil for 20 miles in Gloucester, The trail that they followed jumped 5 foot fences and went under 8 inch spaces. That same day a group of people in Camden, NJ, witnessed the Jersey Devil, upon spotting the people the

Jersey Devil reportedly "barked" at them before taking off into the air and flying way.

The very next day, Wednesday the 19th, a Burlington police officer and the Reverend John Pursell of Pemberton witnessed the Jersey Devil. Reverend John Pursell was quoted as saying "Never saw anything like it before." Groups of people in Haddonfield found tracks that ended abruptly and in Collingswood, NJ, a group of people watched the Jersey Devil fly off towards Moorestown, shortly after, near Moorestown, John Smith of Maple Shade saw the Jersey Devil at the Mount Carmel Cemetery. George Snyder reported seeing the Jersey Devil shortly after Mr. Smith; their descriptions of the creature were almost identical. Later that night in Riverside, NJ, hoof prints where found on roof tops and also, sadly, around a dead puppy.

On Thursday, the 20th, the Jersey Devil was witnessed by the Black Hawk Social Club and also seen by a trolley full of people in Clementon, NJ. When local authorities took descriptions of the beast, the eye witness descriptions matched those of the witnesses from the day before. In Trenton, Councilmen F.P. Weeden heard flapping wings coming from outside his home, upon inspection he discovered strange hoof prints outside of his door. As the day went on Trolley drivers in New Brunswick and Trenton armed themselves to ward off attack, people in the town of Pitman filled local churches and all throughout Delaware Valley farmers where discovering their chickens strewn about their yards, dead, without a mark on them. The West Collingswood Fire Department even went as far as to fire their hoses at the beast. Later that night Mrs. Sorbinski of Camden heard a commotion in her back yard, upon inspection she discovered the Jersey Devil with her dog in its grasp, Mrs. Sorbinski, fearing for her dog's life, began to beat the Jersey Devil with a broom until it dropped her dog and flew off into the night. After hearing the women's screams her neighbors called the police, two officers arrived at her home where over 100 people had gathered.

On Friday, the 21nd, Camden police officer Louis Strehr witnessed the Jersey Devil drinking from his horse's trough. Schools, mills and factories in Gloucester and Hainesport were forced to close because no one would leave their homes. A sketch drawn by Officer Merchant, of Blackwood, NJ, after an encounter with the Jersey Devil matched many eyewitness reports of the creature.

After that flurry of sightings the Jersey Devil was only reported one more time in 1909, however, since then the creature has continued to be sighted by people all over New Jersey. In 1927 a cab driver on his way to Salem suffered a flat tire, upon stopping to fix the flat an upright standing creature landed on the roof of his cab. The creature shook the cab violently, the cab driver ran from the scene, upon his return the creature was no where to be seen. In 1953 Phillip Smith reported seeing the Jersey Devil walking down his street. In 1961 a couple was parked in their car along a road in the Pine Barrens when they heard a load screeching noise outside. Suddenly the roof of their car smashed and the screeching sound was now right on top of them. The couple fled the scene but later returned to witness an unknown creature flying along the tree line making the same screeching noise. In 1966 the Jersey Devil was blamed for the death of 31 ducks, 3 geese, 4 cats and two dogs at a local farm, one of the dogs was a large German Shepard found with its throat ripped out. In 1987 in Vinland, NJ, another German Shepard was found torn apart and the body apparently gnawed upon, the body was located 25 feet from where the dog was chained up, around the body were strange unidentifiable tracks that no one could identify.

There are several theories as to the identity of the New Jersey Devil. One theory is that the creature is actually a Sand Hill Crane, which used to live in the south until driven out by man. The Sand Bill Crane weighs about 12 pounds, is about 4 feet high and has a wingspan of 80 inches. The crane normally avoids people but if confronted will stand and fight, it also has a loud scream which can be heard from a distance, this could explain screams reported by witnesses. One hole in this theory however is that the Sand Hill Crane does not eat meat, which does not explain the killing of live stock. It also does no explain accounts of the creature having a horse like head, bat like wings and a tail.

Some experts, like Professor Bralhopf, believe that the creature is actually a surviving species of Pterodactyl, a prehistoric flying reptile from the Jurassic Period. Supporters of the Pterodactyl theory believe that the creature could have survived in an under ground cavern. This theory does not seem likely, there are few caves large enough to support a large enough breeding population of Pterodactyls for it to have survived millions of years to present day.

There is a small group of people, including Jack F. Boucher, author of Absagami Yesteryear, who believe that the Jersey Devil is as some legends suggest, a deformed child. These people think that Mrs. Leeds gave birth to a disfigured child who she kept locked away in her house. Mrs. Leeds eventually grew sick and could no longer feed the child any longer, out of hunger the child escaped and raided local farms looking for food. Although this would explain the raiding of farms it would not explain the apparent incredible life span of the Jersey Devil. The child would have been 174 years old during the outburst of sightings in 1909 and certainly does not explain accounts of the creature flying.

One last, and less accepted theory is that the Jersey Devil is the very essence of evil, and a harbinger of war. The Jersey Devil has been sighted before the start of the Civil War, the Spanish American War, the Vietnam War and the First World War In 1939 before the start of World War 2, in Mount Holly, NJ; citizens were awakened by the noise of hooves on their roof tops. The Jersey Devil was also sighted on December 7, 1941, right before Pearl Harbor was bombed. Although no one can be sure exactly what the Jersey Devil is thousands of sightings would suggest that something very real haunts the New Jersey Pine Barrens.

The Evidence

Thousands of eyewitness reports and hundreds of footprints suggest that an actually living creature is responsible for the many sightings over the years, however there remains no physical evidence of the creatures existence.

The Sightings

• Joseph Bonaparte, former king of Spain and Brother of the famous Napoleon Bonaparte, reported seeing the Jersey Devil in Bordentown, NJ between 1816 and 1839 while out hunting.

- In the mid 1840's a strange creature with a piercing scream and odd hoof like foot prints began to kill live stock in the area around the Pine Barrens.

- January 16th 1909, Thack Cozzens of Woodbury, NJ, reported seeing a flying creature with glowing eyes flying down the street.

- January 16th 1909, In Bristol, PA, John Mcowen heard and saw the creature on the banks of a channel.

- January 16th 1909, Patrol James Sackville fired on the creature as it flew away screaming.

- January 16th 1909, E.W. Minister, Postmaster for Bristol also reported seeing a bird like creature with a horse head, he reported that the creature also had a piercing scream.

- January 18th 1909, one of the longest sightings of the Jersey Devil was reported by a Mr. and Mrs. Nelson Evans of Gloucester when they were awakened by a strange noise. Upon looking out the winder Mr. Nelson witnessed what he claimed to be the Jersey Devil for 10 minutes. Mr. Evans went on to describe the creature he saw that day:" It was about three feet and half high, with a head like a collie dog and a face like a horse. It had a long neck, wings about two feet long, and its back legs were like those of a crane, and it had horse's hooves. It walked on its back legs and held up two short front legs with paws on them. It didn't use the front legs at all while we were watching. My wife and I were scared, I tell you, but I managed to open the window and say, 'Shoo', and it turned around barked at me, and flew away."

• January 16th 1909, a group of people in Camden, NJ, witnessed the Jersey Devil, upon spotting the people the Jersey Devil reportedly "barked" at them before taking off into the air and flying way.

• January 19th 1909, a Burlington police officer and the Reverend John Pursell of Pemberton witnessed the Jersey Devil. Reverend John Pursell was quoted as saying "Never saw anything like it before."

• January, 20th 1909, the Jersey Devil was witnessed by the Black Hawk Social Club and also seen by a trolley full of people in Clementon, NJ.

• January 20th 1909, Mrs. Sorbinski of Camden heard a commotion in her back yard, upon inspection she discovered the Jersey Devil with her dog in its grasp, Mrs. Sorbinski, fearing for her dog's life, began to beat the Jersey Devil with a broom until it dropped her dog and flew off into the night.

• January 21st 1909, Camden police officer Louis Strehr witnessed the Jersey Devil drinking from his horse's trough.

• In 1927 a cab driver on his way to Salem suffered a flat tire, upon stopping to fix the flat an upright standing creature landed on the roof of his cab. The creature shook the cab violently, the cab driver ran from the scene, upon his return the creature was no where to be seen.

• In 1961 a couple was parked in their car along a road in the Pine Barrens when they heard a load screeching noise outside. Suddenly the roof of their car smashed and the screeching sound was now right on top of them. The couple fled the scene but later returned to witness an unknown creature flying along the tree line making the same screeching noise.

• In 1966 the Jersey Devil was blamed for the death of 31 ducks, 3 geese, 4 cats and two dogs at a local farm, one of the dogs was a large German Shepard found with its throat ripped out.

• In 1987 in Vinland, NJ, another German Shepard was found torn apart and the body apparently gnawed upon, the body was located 25 feet from where the dog was chained up, around the body were strange unidentifiable tracks that no one could identify.

The Stats

• Classification: Unknown

• Size: About 4 feet tall

• Weight: Unknown

• Diet: Carnivorous

• Location: New Jersey

• Movement: Walking and Flight

• Environment: the Pine Barrens, a dense pine forest in New Jersey

Chapter 5: Skunk Ape

Dubbed Skunk Ape due to the foul and unpleasant smell associated with this creature, reports of this hairy bipedal ape like creature have been coming out of southern Florida since the 1920's. Reports of the skunk ape have been reported as far north as Tallahassee, however the majority of Skunk Ape sightings come from in and around the Florida Everglades.

Eye witness descriptions of the creature describe the Skunk Ape as being relatively short in stature, with a reddish brown coat and dangling arms, a description not unlike that of the East African Agogwe or the Sumatran Orang-Pendek. Many reports also describe the Skunk Ape as having glowing red or green eyes; however this is normally attributed to the reflection of a flash light or headlights when the creature is spotted at night.

The earliest published reports of the Skunk Ape are from Suwannee County in 1942 by a man who claimed that one of the creatures hitched a ride on one of his running boards for a little over a half a mile. Since then the popularity of the Skunk Ape in southern Florida has continued to increase, along with the number of sightings. In 1957 two hunters claimed one of the creatures invaded their camp in Big Cypress National Preserve, and between 1963 and 1979 multiple reports came out of Hernando, Pasco and Collier Counties. In 1997 foreign tourists traveling on a bus through the small town of Ochopee reported seeing the Skunk Ape and a naturalist working in the Everglades spotted what he described as a 7 foot primate.

On October 13th, 1998, Naples daily news reported that Collier County campground owner Dave Shealy snapped 27 photos of a 7 foot tall creature walking through the Everglades. Shaely reportedly spend no less than 2 hours a night, every night, over an eight month period, parched up a tree in a home made lookout in hopes of catching a glimpse of the creature. Shaely currently runs the only Skunk Ape Research Center in Florida.

The same year the Dave Shaely took his photographs an Ochopee Fire Chief by the name of Vince Doerr also claimed to have taken a picture of the Skunk Ape in July. Perhaps the most famous photographs of the Skunk Ape were taken anonymously and mailed to the Sarasota Sheriff's Department, Florida, in the year 2000. These photos have become known as the Myakka Skunk-Ape photos. They were accompanied by a letter from a woman claiming to have photographed the creature just outside her backyard, she claimed that she was convinced it was an escaped orangutan.

Many researchers believe that the Skunk Ape is nothing more a small population, or lone, wild orangutans that live the the remote areas of southern Florida and are the descendants of orangutans that escaped from the circus and international airports, or possibly from captivity as an exotic pet. However reports of the creature being as tall as 7 feet would not support the orangutan theory, many believe that the Skunk Ape is a smaller cousin of the Sasquach or Big Foot and is an undiscovered species of primate. The discovery of the Skunk Ape, regardless if it is a previously known species or a new one, would serve to prove that there are still places on this earth animals can live virtually undetected by humans.

The Evidence

There remains no physical evidence of the existence of the Skunk Ape, only eye witness reports and some very interesting photographic material let us know that something out of the ordinary lives in the Florida Everglades and surrounding areas.

The Sightings

- 1942, a man claims that a skunk ape hitched a ride on his running board for a little over half a mile

- 1957, two hunters claim that a Skunk Ape invaded there camp ground at Big Cypress National Preserve

- 1997, tourists on a tour bus traveling through the small town of Ochopee claim to see a skunk ape near the side of the road.

- 1997, a naturalist working in the swamps claims to see a 7 foot tall primate.

- 1998, Dave Shealy takes 27 pictures of what he believes to be the Skunk Ape

- 1998, Ochopee Fire Chief Vince Doerr takes a picture of what is believed to be the Skunk Ape after it crosses the road and enters the forests near his home

- 2000, the Myakka Skunk-Ape photos surface

The Stats

- Classification: Hominid

- Size: upwards of 7 feet tall for the larger males

- Weight: upwards of 450 pounds for the larger males

- Diet: reported to eat both meat and local plant life

- Location: Florida Everglades and surrounding areas

- Movement: walking

- Environment: swamps and forests

Chapter 6: Honey Island Swamp Monster

Honey Island Swamp, a vast swamp land area in southern Louisiana is considered by many naturalists to be one of the most pristine swampland habitats in the United States. Honey Island Swamp is 27 miles in length and seven miles wide, the northern portion consists of vast pine forests which are under the control of the Bogue Chitto National Wildlife Refuge. The middle and bottom portions of the swamp act as a flood plain for the Pearl river, and are managed by the

Louisiana Department of Wildlife and Fisheries. 70,000 acres of this swamp land is permanently protected, very few roads travel into area and is accessible only by boat or foot. The area is a haven for wildlife such as black bear, alligators, white tail deer, feral hogs, rabbits, squirrels, fish, birds and an ever dwindling population of Florida Panther once common across Louisiana. But some believe that lurking the deepest parts of the swamp, parts seldom traveled by man, there lives a monster.

Starting in the early 1960's, as man began to push further into the swamp land, locals began to encounter a large, hair covered, bipedal creature which would come to be known as the Honey Island Swamp Monster. The first document sighting of the creature took place in early august of 1963, when a retired air traffic controller Harlan E. Ford and a friend, Ray Mills, emerged from the deep recesses of Honey Island with an incredible story. The pair of veteran hunters claimed that while out in the swamps they came across a large creature hunched over the body of a dead boar, the strange creature apparently had ripped the boar's throat out. Mr. Ford described the creature as being covered in dingy Grey hair, with longer hair hanging from its head. As the creature glared menacingly at him and his partner, Mr. Ford noticed the creatures clawed hands before it fled into the woods. The two estimated the creature to weight about 400 pounds and stand about 7 feet tall. But what they remembered most were its sickly yellow eyes, set far apart on its skull, and the horrific stench which surrounded the beast.

Although Harlan Ford's and Ray Mills' report was the first official documented sighting of the Honey Island Swamp Monster, stories of this ferocious creature date back hundreds of years. The

Native Americans of the area called the creature Letiche, and described it as "a carnivorous, aquatic-humanoid". They believed that it was once an abandoned child who was raised by alligators in the uncharted regions of the swamp. Cajuns called the creature Loup Carou, which has often been misinterpreted as werewolf. The Honey Island Swamp Monster has been blamed for numerous human and livestock deaths which seem to have plagued the area for decades.

One of the strangest legends surrounding the Honey Island Swamp Monster revolves around a train wreck which allegedly occurred near the Pearl River in the early part of the 20th century. According to this legend, the train was full of exotic animals from a traveling circus, which fled into the swamps after the train derailed. While most of the creatures would soon parish in the harsh swamp land the legend goes on to tell us that a troop of chimpanzees managed to survive and even went as far as to interbreed with alligators. The result was a strange colony of reptilian like mammals.

Some researchers believe that the Honey Island Swamp Monster is related to Bigfoot; the body size certainly is a match as most Bigfoot sightings estimate the creature to be about 7 feet tall and covered in hair. However the tracks found in and around Honey Island Swamp do not resemble tracks collected in the Pacific North West. They are 4 and sometimes 3 toed, much like tracks discovered in southeastern Texas and parts of Florida. Casts made by Harland Ford are about ten to twelve inches long, and have three long thin toes set next to each other and a fourth set back on the inside, rather like a thumb. Some researchers believe that this could be an isolated population of big foot, cut off from other big foot they where forced to breed with members of the same family. When inbreeding takes place, the first area to be effect with genetic deformities are fingers and toes, this theory may explaining why the Honey Island Monster and other southern hominids tracks only have 3 or 4 toes. The mystery of the Honey Island Swamp Monster continues to this day, with a hand full of eye witnesses reporting encounters each year, one thing is for sure, if there where ever an area to hide a large creature from human eyes Honey Island Swamp would be the place.

The Evidence

To date there is no physical evidence of the Honey Island Swamp Monster, in 1978 Alan Lamdsburg Company, producers of the popular TV program; IN SEARCH OF did a segment on the Honey island Swamp Monster. Some plaster casts of the creature's foot prints have also been gathered as proof, however with out solid physical evidence modern science will never accept the Honey Island Swamp Monster as fact.

The Sightings

• 1963, Harlen Ford and Ray Mills report what would be come the first documented accounts of the creature.

• 1973, a guide was traveling down a bayou in a small boat when it struck something in the water. The guide stopped to see what it was when he saw a creature swim to shore, climb out the water then walk into the woods on two legs.

• A local man, Ted Williams describes two encounters with the creature:

First time I ever saw it, it was standing plum still like a stump. I stopped
and realized it wasn't a stump and it wasn't supposed to be there. When
I stopped it ran. It was dark gray, about seven foot high, it jumped a
bayou [a bayou is the southern equivalent of a stream, except the water
moves so slow it may not even appear to have a flow], that was the first
time I saw it. The next time I seen him was swimming the river [Pearl
River], two of them, one was bigger than the other and faster than the
other and they swam just like a human with them long overhead strokes.
I tried to get one of them to look at me and the other one ran off and
the other one wouldn't look at me. I could've shot it but I wouldn't on
account it wouldn't look at me. It looked too much like a human too
me, broad shoulders, arms hanging down below its knees, hands looked
almost like a humans."

• Barry Ford describes his encounter to the In Search Of crew:

"My wife and I were going on a fishing trip about four years ago and at
about 9:00pm [the video shows them camping in the swamp] that night I
heard this peculiar noise, a scream down the river, I'd say about a half a
mile away. My wife wanted me to build a fire so I was out gathering
wood, and it screamed again, this time it was closer, maybe three
hundred yards. That's when it really scared her, it scared me but I tried
not to let her know it scared me, so I went ahead and kept building fires
[video shows them building small fires around their camp] and less than
ten minutes later it screamed again and this time it was right on top of
us. It almost shook the leaves off the trees."

• Harlen Ford retells another encounter with the creature:

"One evening late, just about dark a friend and I we encountered eyes, they were a yellow or amber color set real wide apart, so this friend of mine, Jim Hartzog, he took a gun and went into this area to try to kill whatever it was and he says he came face to face with this thing. It looked like an ape about seven feet tall, and he fired on it. He said when he did the eyes went away. It most likely turned and ran, he shot at it one more time. So we went back the next day to look for signs and blood but we didn't find any. We figured Jim missed it that night.

The Stats

- Classification: Hominid

- Size: Larger males reach heights upwards of 7 feet

- Weight: Larger males reach weights in excess of 400 pounds

- Diet: Reports suggest this creature is carnivorous

- Location: Honey Island Swamp, Louisiana

- Movement: Bipedal

- Environment: Swampy flood plains and dense pine forests

Chapter 7: Yeren

     The Yeren, or wild man, is a yet undiscovered bipedal hominid reported to reside in the mountainous and forested regions of China. The Yeren's height often ranges between 6 to 9 feet and is said to be covered from head to toe in reddish brown hair. It is said to have a sloping forehead which rises up above the eyes like a humans, its eyes are set deep and its whole face, with the exception of its nose and ears, is covered in short hairs. The Yeren's arms hang below its knees; its hands are about half a foot long and its thumbs only slightly separate from its fingers.

The Yeren has been a part of the folklore of southern and central China for centuries. Ancient Chinese literary works and folk legends include references to big hairy man like creatures which live in the vast forests of the Quinling Bashan Shennongjia, a mountain region of central China. Roughly 2,000 years ago, during the Warring States period, Qu Yuan, the statesman poet of the State of Chu, referred in his verses to mountain ogres. His home was just south of Shennongjia, in what is today the Zigui country of the Hubei province. During the Tang Dynasty, the historian Li Yanshou, in his Southern History, describes a band of hairy men in the region of modern Jiangling country, also in the Hubei province.

The Hubei province its self is home to the Shennongjia Mountains, an area approximately 1,250 square miles that is comprised of steep, rugged mountains reaching up to 8,000 feet with peaks as high as 10,000 feet. Areas above 6,000 feet retain a temperature similar to early winter even while the surrounding lower lying hills swelter. This constant, year round, cool climate has resulted in the growth and survival of a unique and diverse ecosystem. The area is home to rare and exotic woods, including the arrow bamboo which makes high quality paper and provides food for China's giant pandas. This region is also full of plant life sometimes referred to as living fossils, including the metasequoia, the dove tree and the Chinese tulip tree. The Shennongjia region contains several rare animals as well, including a white bear, the giant panda, the takin and the golden monkey, some of these species are found no where else in the world and sightings of the Yeren are most frequent in this diverse area as well.

Regional officials have recorded nearly four hundred sightings in and around this region since the 1920's; with a number of these sightings being reported by very credible eyewitnesses. In 1940, biologist Wang Tselin claimed to have examined the corpse of a Yeren that had been killed in the Gansu region. He stated that the specimen was a female, over 6 feet tall, with striking features that appeared to be a cross between ape and human. Also Geologist Fan Jingquan reported seeing a pair of Yeren, what he thought was a mother and son, in the forests of the Shanxi province in 1950.

In 1961, a team of road builders reportedly killed a female Yeren in the forests of Xishuang Banna. Officials from the Chinese Academy of Sciences where called out to investigate the creature, however when they arrived the body had disappeared. The team of scientists concluded that the creature, which was described as approximately 4 feet tall, had been an ordinary gibbon. But twenty years later, a journalist who claimed to have been involved in the investigation came forward to claim that the creature killed was not a gibbon, but an unknown animal of human shape.

On May 14th 1976, six men from the Shennongjia forestry region were driving along a highway near Chunshuy, a village between Fangxian country and Shennongjia, when they came across a strange tailless creature covered in reddish fur illuminated in the headlights of their car. This incident sparked a great degree of public interest and lead to a group of scientists and the army mounting several expeditions into the forest, including one massive expedition of over 100 members comprised of scientists, photographers and special infiltration teams of soldiers with rifles, tranquilizer dart guns, tape recorders and hunting dogs. Though the search did not bring back any solid proof, at one point during the expedition a search party did encountered a Yeren, but as they moved closer to capture the creature an anxious solider reportedly shot himself in the leg, the shot brought expedition members from all directions to their location and presumably scared the Yeren away.

One of the closest thing to solid physical evidence of the Yeren's existence was brought to light in 1980 in the form of the preserved hands and feet of an unknown hominid creature. Reportedly, villagers had killed the Yeren in the Zhejiang province in 1957, and a biology teacher had the foresight to remove and preserve the extremities. However upon examination of the hands and feet, researcher Zhou Guoxing, though not 100% sure, announced that they had come from a large macaque monkey.

Another large scale expedition to find the Yeren was launched in 1980 and operated until 1985 near Songbai in the Shennongjia Forest. More than two hundred footprints were discovered and documented on Mount Quiangdao. These foot prints where roughly 18 inches in length with the average stride between footprints being 6 feet. Eyewitness accounts where also recorded but no Yeren was captured or photographed.

The majority of modern Yeren researchers believe the creature to be a surviving specimen of Gigantopithecus blacki, a genus of ape that lived in the area as recently as 100 thousand years ago. Based of the slim fossil evidence, mainly huge molars and jaw fragments, Gigantopithecus was likely 9 feet tall and would have weighed around 700 pounds. Other researchers believe the Yeren to be an undiscovered species of Orangutan which evolved over thousands of years to walk as a biped. And still others believe that sightings of the Yeren are nothing more than the misidentification of already known animals such as the rare golden monkey or gibbon whose face it thought to look quite human like.

The Evidence

As with most large hair covered hominids the majority of physical evidence comes from casts of footprints found in areas where the creature has been reported, however some evidence also includes hair samples and droppings. In 1988 several hairs, thought to have come from a Yeren, where examined by the animal biology department at Shanghai's Huadong Normal University under the supervision of biology professor Liu Minzhuang. Atomic and chemical analyses of the hairs showed that the levels of calcium, iron and copper to be higher in the Yeren hair sample compared to nine other samples which included human, black bears, golden monkeys and orangutans.

The Sightings

In 1940, biologist Wang Tselin claimed to have examined the corpse of a Yeren that had been killed in the Gansu region.

In 1950, geologist Fan Jingquan reported seeing a pair of Yeren, what he thought was a mother and son, in the forests of the Shanxi province.

In 1961, a team of road builders reportedly killed a female Yeren in the forests of Xishuang Banna.

On May 14th 1976, six men from the Shennongjia forestry region were driving along a highway near Chunshuy, a village between Fangxian country and Shennongjia, when they came across a strange tailless creature covered in reddish fur which was illuminated in the headlights of their car.

In 1999, a hunter reported seeing a huge fast moving creature covered in long red hair in the hubei province's Shennongjia Nature Reserve.

The Stats

- Classification: Hominid

- Size: 6 to 9 feet tall

- Weight: Unknown

- Diet: Unknown

- Location: China

- Movement: Bipedal walking

- Environment: Mountainous Regions

Chapter 8: Chupacabra

The chupacabra is a creature said to inhabit parts of the Latin America, associated particularly with Puerto Rico, where it was first reported, Mexico, Chile, Brazil and the United States, especially in the latter's Latin American communities. Other reports have also noted the Chupacabra in regions throughout North America, from Miami to Maine. Perhaps this creature has been confused with other possible cryptids and summed up into just one term.

The name translates in Portuguese and Spanish literally as "goat-sucker". This name comes from the creature's reported habit of attacking and drinking the blood of livestock, especially goats. Sightings began in Puerto Rico in the early 1990s, and have since been reported as far north as Maine, and as far south as Chile. Though some argue that the chupacabras may be real creatures, mainstream scientists and experts generally contend that the chupacabra is a legendary creature, or a type of urban legend.

The legend of El Chupacabra began in 1947, when Puerto Rican newspapers El Vocero and El Nuevo Dia began reporting that local farmers livestock where being killed, such as birds, horses, and as its name implies, goats. While at first it was suspected that the killings were done randomly by some members of a Satanic cult, eventually these killings spread around the island, hundreds of farms reported loss of animal life. These strange killings had one pattern in common, each of the animals found dead had two punctured holes around its neck.

Soon after the animal deaths in Puerto Rico, other animal deaths were reported in other countries, such as the Dominican Republic, Argentina, Bolivia, Chile, Colombia, Honduras, El Salvador, Panama, Peru, Brazil, the United States and, most notably, Mexico. Both in Puerto Rico and Mexico, "El Chupacabra" gained urban legend status, Chupacabra stories began to be released in American and Hispanic newscasts across the United States, and Chupacabra merchandise, such as T-shirts and baseball caps, were sold. The Chupacabra is generally treated as a product of mass hysteria, though the animal mutilations are sometimes real.

Like many cases of such mutilations, however, it has been argued that they are often not as mysterious as they might first appear, and in fact, a series of tests showcased by the National Geographic

Channel in a show about the Chupacabra pointed to the obvious conclusion that every single "animal mutilation" can be explained by either people killing them or, more likely, other animals eating them.

The loss of blood may be explained by insects drinking it. Certain South American rain forest natives believe in the "mosquito man", a mythical creature of their folklore that pre-dates modern Chupacabra sightings. The Mosquito-Man sucks the blood from animals through his long nose, like a big mosquito. Some say mosquito-man and the chupacabra are one and the same.

One story states that in September of 2006, a hotel employee named Valerie Pauls of Albuquerque, New Mexico was startled by a hissing noise upon arriving for work at about 7:00 in the morning. She glanced up to the sixth floor roof of the Amerisuites Hotel. She saw two glowing red eyes peering down upon her. The creature resembled a gargoyle, and smelled of sulfur. The creature terrified Ms. Pauls as it continued hissing and flashing neon colors.

She became dizzy and disoriented. She managed to return to her vehicle as the alleged Chupacabra descended upon her vehicle. The creature broke the windshield before leaping back unto the roof of the hotel and vanishing. Notable sightings in the United States include one reported by multiple eye-witnesses in Calaveras County, California, and at a recent birthday celebration of a Development Team member of a local charity in Houston, Texas.

In July 2004, a rancher near San Antonio, Texas, killed a hairless, dog-like creature which was attacking his livestock. This creature is now known as the Elmendorf Creature. It was later determined to be a canine of some sort, most likely a coyote, with demodectic mange. In October 2004, two animals which closely resemble the Elmendorf Creature were observed in the same area. The first was dead, and a local zoologist who was called to identify the animal noticed the second while she was traveling to the location where the first was found. Specimens were studied by biologists in Texas. The creatures are thought to have been canines of undetermined species with skin problems and facial deformities.

In 2005, Isaac Espinoza reportedly spent close to $6 million of his own money trying to track down the Chupacabra. He lived in the jungles of South America for eight months with a team of researchers, video and print journalists and local guides. During the course of the expedition the team had several close encounters with a creature that the researchers were not able to identify. The team was able to capture several of their encounters with the creature on film and it has all been turned over to the University of Texas for analysis. Hugo Mata, a professor of cryptozoology at the University of Texas, has said the hair and skin samples submitted by the team do not match any known species for that part of the world.

In Albuquerque, New Mexico, A 42 year old woman, Rebecca Tuggle, was on the way to her car when she heard a mysterious hissing noise. As she turned around she was terrified to see a creature partially resembling a lizard, a kangaroo, and a bat, with "rainbow-colored" spines running down its back. The creature stood 3 to 4 feet tall and grunted at her. The creature's hissing noise nauseated her and she nearly fainted. As with other sightings, the eyes were said to glow red and the animal smelled of a sulfuric substance. The Chupacabra has often been spotted in Michigan. A recent un confirmed sighting occurred in Grand Haven, when a 42-year-old man claimed he saw it suck the blood out of a cat.

A famous appearance in the city of Varginha, Brazil, known as the "Varginha incident", is sometimes attributed to the Chupacabra, although cryptozoologists more frequently associate the incident with extraterrestrials. In 1997, an explosion of Chupacabra sightings in Brazil where reported in Brazilian newspapers. One report came from a police officer, who claimed to get a nauseous feeling when he saw a dog-like chupacabra in a tree. Recently, there has been a surge of Chupacabra sightings in the United States, specifically in the suburbs of Washington, D.C., and outside of the Philadelphia, Pennsylvania area. However, controversy exists whether these chupacabra sightings are legitimate.

In Coleman, Texas, a farmer named Reggie Lagow caught an unknown animal in a trap he set up after the deaths of a number of his chickens and turkeys. The animal appeared to be a mix between a hairless dog, a rat and a kangaroo. The mystery animal was reported to Texas Parks and Wildlife in hopes of determining what it was, but Lagow said in a September 17th, 2006, phone interview with John Adolfi, founder of the Lost World Museum, that the "critter was caught on a Tuesday and thrown out in Thursday's trash."

In September of 2006, in High Rolls, New Mexico, near Alamogordo, A roper Trey Rogers spotted what he believed was the El Chupacabra. He was out in the forest with his paint ball gun looking for game when he spotted a medium sized brown reddish-animal that had spikes down its back and wings on its side. Before Trey could get a shot it took off at the speed or fastest than the quickest rabbit. It was the fastest thing Trey had ever seen.

In April of 2006, MosNews reported that the chupacabra was spotted in Russia for the first time. Reports from Central Russia beginning in March 2005 tell of a beast that kills animals and sucks out their blood. Thirty-two turkeys were killed and drained overnight. Reports later came from neighboring villages when 30 sheep were killed and had their blood drained. Finally eyewitnesses were able to describe the Chupacabra.

In mid-August 2006, Michelle O'Donnell of Turner, Maine, described an "evil looking" dog-like creature with fangs found along side a road, apparently struck by a car, but it was otherwise unidentifiable. Photographs were taken and several witness reports seem to be in relative agreement that the creature was canine in appearance, but unlike any dog or wolf in the area. The carcass was picked clean by vultures before experts could examine it. For years, residents of Maine have reported a mysterious creature and a string of dog maulings.

On September 2006, the Lost World Museum acquired the remains of what may be a Chupacabra. Spotted, hunted and killed in late August 2006, 15 yr. old Geordie Decker and 16 yr. old Josh Underwood of Berkshire, New York handed over the bones of a small fox like beast that hopped, had yellow eyes and an orange strip of hair going down its almost bald gray back, to Museum owner John Adolfi.

Its bones are currently on display on the Lost World Museum's web site while further examination and investigation continues. Stacey Womack, dog breeder and former veterinarian tech assistant, Lufkin,

Texas: "My mother was just sort of hysterical because they had killed something under the house and they did not know what it was. I thought, 'This is the most ridiculous thing I've ever heard.'

They don't know whether it's a coyote or a dog?! I told my mother I would come out there and bring my digital camera. About one-quarter mile from my mother's house, I had to hit my breaks because an animal crossed the road in front of me and it was running with its head down and its tail down and it did not have any hair. It was a strange looking sight and my daughter-in-law was with me and she wanted to know if it was a wolf.

I told her it wasn't a wolf and it was too large for a fox. So, we went on to my mother's house and went around to the back and there was the same animal an animal identical to what ran across the road. It was on the ground after they had just killed it and there was almost no blood. It was just red where the shot had went in (the eye). I was just totally dumbfounded when I saw it. At first glance, you would think of a deer's head on a kangaroo's body. The ears were real thick and large. It did not have any hair on it. The skin tissue was necrotic. It was just awful. I did not know what it was."

Descriptions of the physical appearance of each specimen can resemble descriptions of other reports, or be completely different from other Chupacabra descriptions. Differences in descriptions are too wide to be attributed to differences in the perceptions of the observers, causing cryptozoologists to speculate that Chupacabra reports may in fact be attributable to several species. Although they have different appearances, Chupacabra descriptions have several common traits. The following 3 descriptions of the Chupacabra are the most commonly reported:

The first and most common form is a lizard-like being, appearing to have leathery or scaly greenish-gray skin and sharp spines or quills running down its back. This form stands approximately 3 to 4 feet high, and stands and hops in a similar fashion to a kangaroo. In at least one sighting, the creature hopped 20 feet. This variety is said to have a dog or panther-like nose and face, a forked tongue protruding from it, large fangs, and to hiss and screech when alarmed, as well as leave a sulfuric stench behind. When it screeches, some reports note that the Chupacabra's eyes glow an unusual red, then give the witnesses nausea.

The second variety bears a resemblance to a wallaby or dog standing on its hind legs. It stands and hops as a kangaroo, and it has coarse fur with grayish facial hair. The head is similar to a dog's, and its mouth has large teeth.

The third form is described as a strange breed of wild dog. This form is mostly hairless, has a pronounced spinal ridge, unusually pronounced eye sockets, teeth, and claws. This animal is said to be the result of interbreeding between several populations of wild dogs, though enthusiasts claim that it might be an example of a dog-like reptile. The account during the year 2001 in Nicaragua of a chupacabra's corpse being found supports the conclusion that it is simply a strange breed of wild dog. The alleged corpse of the animal was found in Tolapa, Nicaragua, and forensically analyzed at UNAN-Leon. Pathologists at the University found that it was just an unusual-looking dog. There are very striking morphological differences between different breeds of dog, which can easily account for the strange characteristics.

Some reports claim the Chupacabra's red eyes have the ability to hypnotize and paralyze their prey, leaving the prey animal mentally stunned, allowing the chupacabra to suck the animal's blood at its leisure. The effect is similar to the bite of the vampire bat, or of certain snakes or spiders that stun their prey with venom. Unlike conventional predators, the Chupacabras sucks all the animal's blood, and sometimes organs, through a single hole or two holes in the creatures neck.

Many residents of South America have reported sightings of El Chupacabras, and although various, the descriptions share some significant likenesses. In many reports, accounts include the visible inflation of the stomach region, after El Chupacabra has been feeding. The appearance of the animal changes when an internal bladder-like organ fills with the blood of its prey. Furthermore, with almost all the reported sightings witnesses have reported large protruding fangs. These fangs are suspected to be hollow and be the vehicles for the blood on which it feeds.

Chupacabras have been described as similar in appearance to gargoyles, so it has been theorized that the creatures were seen in Medieval Europe. According to this theory, gargoyles were carved to resemble Chupacabras, to keep the public, and sometimes believed to keep evil spirits, afraid of any place with gargoyles. Some cryptozoologists speculate that chupacabras are alien creatures.

Chupacabras are widely described as otherworldly, and, according to one witness report, NASA may be involved with this particular alien's residency on earth. The witness reported that NASA passed through an area in Latin America, with a trailer that was thought to contain an incarcerated creature. There have also been UFOs seen where Chupacabras have been at the same time on occasion. Others speculate that the creature is an escaped pet of alien visitors that wandered off while its master was visiting Earth. The Chupacabra does have a slight resemblance to the Greys, a form of alien said to visit earth, which could mean that they are somehow related.

Some people in the island of Puerto Rico believe that the Chupacabras were a genetic experiment from some United States' government agency, which escaped from a secret laboratory in El Yunque, a mountain in the east part of the island when the laboratory was damaged during a severe storm in the early 1990s. The US military have had a large presence across Puerto Rico since the 1930s, with bases on the island used as Research and Development facilities, amongst other things, up to the present day.

The lethal agent orange chemicals were tested by the US on the crops of Puerto Rico in widespread crop-spraying operations, all performed without notifying local people or farmers, and the efficacy and safety of contraceptive medicines was also secretly tested on islanders who had no knowledge of their 'guinea pig' status at all.

Another possibility would involve giant vampire bats of which a few fossils have been found in South-America. An alternative explanation is that the creatures are not real at all, and the sightings are either a product of superstition and imagination, or simply other animals that have been wrongly identified. There is only one thing we know for sure about El Chupacabra, that is that we know nothing about what the creature might actually be.

The Evidence

Evidence of El Chupacabra is limited to numerous sightings and strange, canine like, carcasses. Sightings of the Chupacabra have been reported all over the world, from Russia to Maine to Puerto Rico, corpses of unidentified canine like creatures have also been discovered in area's the Chupacabra have been spotted. These bodies are normally attributed to sickly coyotes with severe cases of mange. Several photo's of the alleged creature have surfaced however most have been disproved as hoaxes.

The Sightings

Hundreds, if not thousands of Chupacabra sightings or creatures described like one of the three versions of the beast have been reported world wide. This creature seems to be on the rise as far as sightings are concerned and seems to be spreading globally. Below are just a handful of the well documented accounts that were reported.

In Albuquerque, New Mexico, A 42 year old woman (Rebecca Tuggle) was on the way to her car when she heard a mysterious hissing noise. As she turned around she was terrified to see a creature partially resembling a lizard, a kangaroo, and a bat, with "rainbow-colored" spines running down its back. The creature stood 3-4' tall and grunted at her. The creature's hissing noise nauseated her and she nearly fainted. As with other sightings, the eyes were said to glow red and the animal smelled of a sulfuric substance The chupacabra has often been spotted in Michigan. A recent sighting occurred in Grand Haven, when a 42-year-old man claimed he saw it suck the blood out of a cat.

In the fall of 1996 our founder, Jay Correia, had a vivid close encounter with a creature he believes is a Chupacabra or version of it in a cemetery behind his house after clearing through some woods. The encounter lasted roughly 30-45 seconds when a kangaroo like creature with the face of a dog which had course short fur was seen going through a trash heap. The creature turned, snarled, looked directly at him, and then wobble hopped its way into the forest and seemingly vanished. To read the full story Click Here.

In 1997, an explosion of chupacabra sightings in Brazil was reported in Brazilian newspapers. One report came from a police officer, who claimed to get a nauseous feeling when he saw a dog-like chupacabra in a tree. Recently, there has been a surge of chupacabra sightings in the United States, specifically in the suburbs of Washington, D.C., and outside of the Philadelphia, Pennsylvania area.

July 2004, a rancher near San Antonio, Texas, killed a hairless, dog-like creature which was attacking his livestock. This creature is now known as the Elmendorf Creature. It was later determined to be a canine of some sort, most likely a coyote, with demodectic mange.

October 2004, two animals which closely resemble the Elmendorf Creature were observed in the same area. The first was dead, and a local zoologist who was called to identify the animal noticed the second while she was traveling to the location where the first was found. Specimens were studied by biologists in Texas. The creatures are thought to have been canines of undetermined species with skin problems and facial deformities.

2005, Isaac Espinoza reportedly spent close to $6 million of his own money trying to track down the chupacabra. He lived in the jungles of South America for eight months with a team of researchers, video and print journalists and local guides. During the course of the expedition the team had several close encounters with a creature that the researchers were not able to identify. The team was able to capture several of their encounters with the creature on film and it has all been turned over to the University of Texas for analysis.

September 17th, 2006, In Coleman, Texas, a farmer named Reggie Lagow caught an unknown animal in a trap he set up after the deaths of a number of his chickens and turkeys. The animal appeared to be a mix between a hairless dog, a rat and a kangaroo. The mystery animal was reported to be to Texas Parks and Wildlife in hopes of determining what it was.

September of 2006, in High Rolls, New Mexico, near Alamogordo, A roper Trey Rogers spotted what he believed was the El Chupacabra. He was out in the forest with his paint ball gun looking for game when he spotted a medium sized brown reddish-animal that had spikes down its back and wings on its side. Before Trey could get a shot it took off at the speed or fastest than the quickest rabbit. It was the fastest thing Trey had ever seen.

September of 2006, a hotel employee named Valerie Pauls of Albuquerque, New Mexico was startled by a hissing noise upon arriving for work at about 7:00 in the morning. She glanced up to the sixth floor roof of the Amerisuites Hotel. She saw two glowing red eyes peering down upon her. The creature resembled a gargoyle, and smelled of sulfur The creature terrified Ms. Pauls as it continued hissing and flashing neon colors. She became dizzy and disoriented. She managed to return to her vehicle as the alleged Chupacabra descended upon her vehicle. The creature broke the windshield before leaping back up unto the roof of the hotel and vanishing.

April of 2006, MosNews reported that the chupacabra was spotted in Russia for the first time. Reports from Central Russia beginning in March 2005 tell of a beast that kills animals and sucks out their blood. Thirty-two turkeys were killed and drained overnight. Reports later came from neighboring villages when 30 sheep were killed and had their blood drained. Finally eyewitnesses were able to describe the chupacabra.

August 2006, Michelle O'Donnell of Turner, Maine, described an "evil looking" dog-like creature with fangs found along side a road, apparently struck by a car, but it was otherwise unidentifiable.

September 2006, the Lost World Museum acquired the remains of what may be a Chupacabra. Spotted, hunted and killed in late August 2006, 15 yr. old Geordie Decker and 16 yr. old Josh Underwood of Berkshire, New York handed over the bones of a small fox like beast that hopped, had yellow eyes and an orange strip of hair going down its almost bald gray back, to Museum owner John Adolfi. Its bones are currently on display on the Lost World Museum's web site while further examination and investigation continues.

Spring 2007, a series of supposed chupacabra sightings popped up in remote villages in the South American country of Chile. Hundreds of sightings are now reported annually.

The Stats

- Classification: Unknown / Hybrid

- Size:3 – 5 Feet Tall

- Weight: Unknown (estimated 65-130lbs)

- Diet: The Blood of Small Animals and Livestock

- Location: World Wide

- Movement: Walking and in some cases Flying

- Environment: Wooded Area's surrounding farm land

Chapter9: Werewolf

According to mythology and folklore the Werewolf, also sometimes called a Lycanthropy or wolf man, is a person who shape shifts his or her self into a wolf, either at will, by using a form of magic, or after being placed under a curse. The term Werewolf was most likely derived from the Old English word, wer and wulf, wer meaning man and wulf meaning wolf, so Werewolf literally translates into man wolf.

The Greek term Lycanthropy is also commonly used for the physical transformation of the man into the wolf and vies versa. The medieval chronicler Gervase of Tilbury associated this transformation with the appearance of the full moon, but that concept was rarely associated with the Werewolf until the idea was picked up by modern fiction writers. These modern writers also gave us the idea that the Werewolf can be killed by a silver bullet, although this was not a feature of folk legends. In fact much of the information found in modern day Werewolf movies is not based off of the old legends, however the legend of the Werewolf has been around for centuries.

Many European countries and cultures have stories of Werewolves, this list includes France's, loup-garou, The Greek lycanthropes, Spain's hombre lobo, Bulgaria's varkolak and vulkodlak, Czech Republic's vlkodlak, Serbia's vukodlak, Russia's oboroten', Ukraine's vovkulak, vurdalak, vovkun or pereverten' , Croatia's vukodlak, Poland's wilkolak, Romania's vârcolac, Scotland's werewolf or wulver, England's werewolf, Ireland's faoladh or conriocht, Germany's Werwolf, Holland's weerwolf, Denmark, Sweden and Norway's Varulv, Norway and Iceland's kveld-ulf or varúlfur, Galicia's lobisón, Portugal and Brazil's lobisomem, Lithuania's vilkolakis and vilkatlakis, Latvia's vilkatis and vilkacis, Andorra's home llop, Estonia's libahunt, Finland's ihmissusi and vironsusi, and Italy's lupo mannaro. All of these locations had there own stories of wolf men, and in northern Europe there were tales of people who could change into other animals including bears and wolves.

In Greek mythology the story of Lycaon supplies one of the earliest examples of a werewolf legend. According to one telling of the legend, Lycaon, king of Arcadia during the time of the ancient Greeks, was transformed into a wolf as a result of eating human flesh; another telling of the Lycaon legend states that he tried to buy the favor of Zeus by offering him the flesh of a young child, repulsed Zeus punished Lycoan by turning him into a wolf.

In Norse mythology, the legends of ulfhednar mentioned in the Vatnsdœla saga, there were vicious fighters, analogous to the better known berserker, who dressed in wolf hides and where said to channel the spirits of these animals, enhancing their own power and ferocity in battle. They were even said to be immune to pain and would kill viciously in battle, like a wild animal. In Latvian mythology, the Vilkacis was a person who would changed into a wolf like monster.

Many of the Werewolves in European tradition were innocent and God fearing persons, who suffered through the witchcraft of others, or simply from an unhappy fate, and who as wolves behaved in a truly touching fashion, fawning upon and protecting their benefactors. In Marie de France's poem Bisclaveret, the nobleman Bisclavret, for reasons not described in the lai, had to transform into a wolf every week. When his treacherous wife stole his clothing, needed to restore his human form, he escaped the king's wolf hunt by imploring the king for mercy, and accompanied the king thereafter.

His behavior at court was so gentle and harmless than when his wife and her new husband appeared at court, his attack on them was taken as evidence of reason to hate them, and the truth was revealed. Other individuals similar to this was the hero of William and the Werewolf, translated from French into English about 1350, and the numerous princes and princesses, knights and ladies, who appear temporarily in beast form in the German fairy tales, or Märchen.

Some werewolf lore is based on documented events. The Beast of Gévaudan was a creature that reportedly terrorized the general area of the former province of Gévaudan, in today's Lozère department, in the Margeride Mountains in south central France, in the general time frame of 1764 to 1767. It was often described as a giant wolf and was said to attack livestock and humans indiscriminately. In the late 1990s, a string of man eating wolf attacks were reported in Uttar Pradesh, India. Frightened people claimed, among other things, that the wolves were Werewolves.

Historical legends describe a wide variety of methods for becoming a werewolf. One of the simplest was the removal of clothing and putting on a belt made of wolf skin, probably a substitute for the assumption of an entire animal skin which also is frequently described. In other cases the body is rubbed with a magic salve. To drink water out of the footprint of the animal in question or to drink from certain enchanted streams were also considered effectual modes of accomplishing metamorphosis.

Olaus Magnus says that the Livonian Werewolves were initiated by draining a cup of specially prepared beer and repeating a set formula. Another theory is to be born on the 24th of December, and the child shall be born a werewolf. The most common modern belief is to be directly bitten by a werewolf, where the saliva enters the blood stream. Becoming a werewolf simply by being bitten by another werewolf as a form of contagion is common in modern fiction, but rare in legend, in which werewolf attacks seldom left the victim alive to transform.

According to The Book of Werewolves by Sabine Baring-Gould, a Russian spell to transform into a werewolf, referred to as Oborot in the text, is as follows: "He who desires to become an oborot, let him seek in the forest a hewn-down tree, let him stab it with a small copper knife, and walk round the tree, repeating the following incantation:"

On the sea, on the ocian, on the island, on Bujan,

On the empty pasture gleams the moon, on an ashstock lying

In a green wood, in a gloomy vale.

Towards the Stock wandereth a shaggy wolf,

Horned cattle seeking for his sharp white fangs,

But the wolf enters not the forest,

But the wolf dives not into the shadowy vale,

Moon, moon, gold horned moon,

Check the flight of bullets, blunt the hunters' knives,

Break the shepherds' cudels,

On men, all creeping things,

They may not catch the Grey wolf,

That they may not rend his warm skin!

My word is binding, more binding than sleep,

More binding than the promise of a hero!

"Then he springs thrice over the tree and runs into the forest, transformed into a wolf."

In Galician, Portuguese and Brazilian folklore, it is the seventh of the son, but sometimes the seventh child, a boy, after a line of six daughters, who becomes a werewolf. In Portugal, the seventh daughter is supposed to become a witch and the seventh son a werewolf; the seventh son often gets the Christian name, Bento, Portuguese form of Benedict, meaning blessed, as this is believed to prevent him from becoming a werewolf later in life.

In Brazil, the seventh daughter become a headless, the head being replaced with fire, horse called Mula-sem-cabeça. The belief in the curse of the seventh son was so extended in Northern Argentina, that seventh sons were often abandoned, ceded in adoption or killed. A law from 1920 decreed that the President of Argentina is to be the godfather of every seventh son. Thus, the State gives that son a gold medal during his baptism and a scholarship until his 21st year. This ended the abandonments, but it is still traditional that the President godfathers seventh sons.

Various methods also existed for removing the beast shape. The simplest was the act of the enchanter, operating either on himself or on a victim, and another was the removal of the animal belt or skin. To kneel in one spot for a hundred years, to be reproached with being a werewolf, to be saluted with the sign of the cross, or addressed thrice by baptismal name, to be struck three blows on the forehead with a knife, or to have at least three drops of blood drawn have also been mentioned as possible cures. Many European folk tales include throwing an iron object over or at the werewolf, to make it reveal its human form.

A recent theory has been proposed to explain werewolf episodes in Europe in the 18th and 19th centuries. Ergot, which causes a form of food borne illness, is a fungus that grows in place of rye grains in wet growing seasons after very cold winters. Ergot poisoning usually affects whole towns or at least poor areas of towns and results in hallucinations, mass hysteria and paranoia, as well as convulsions and sometimes death., the drug LSD can be derived from ergot. Ergot poisoning has been proposed as both a cause of an individual believing that he or she is a werewolf and of a whole town believing that they had seen a werewolf. However, this theory is controversial and not well accepted.

Some modern researchers have tried to use conditions such as rabies, hypertrichosis, and excessive hair growth over the entire body, or porphyria, an enzyme disorder with symptoms including hallucinations and paranoia, as an explanation for Werewolf beliefs. Congenital erythropoietin porphyria has clinical features which include photosensitivity. Making it so sufferers can only go out at night, hairy hands and face, poorly healing skin, pink urine, and reddish color to the teeth.

There is also a rare mental disorder called clinical Lycanthropy, in which an affected person has a delusional belief that he or she is transforming into another animal, although not always a wolf or werewolf. Others believe Werewolf legends arose as a part of shamanism and totem animals in primitive and nature based cultures. The term therianthropy has been adopted to describe a spiritual concept in which the individual believes he or she has the spirit or soul, in whole or in part, of a non-human animal.

With so many different theories and assumptions as to the origins of the Werewolf and its many legends we many never truly know just where it all started. But the fact remains that something did start the legend, a legend which spread over the globe. Was it just a case of mistaken Identity, of a large rogue wolf which prayed upon small villages or could it have been as legend suggests, an actually transformation of man to beast.

The Evidence

No physical evidence exists to date that would prove the existence of the Werewolf, in the present or in the past.

The Sightings

The only sightings of werewolves reported took place during medieval sieges or came up as folklore and story typically involving stressful time periods. No modern day accounts of actual true werewolf sightings have been reported.

The Stats

- Classification: Hybrid

- Size: Varies greatly depending on the legend and region

- Weight: Unknown

- Diet: Carnivorous

- Location: World Wide

- Movement: Walking

- Environment: Judging from the many legends, it would appear that the Werewolf can exist in almost any environment on earth.

Chapter 10: Lizard Men

The Term Lizard Men is not specific to one specific cryptid; instead it is used to describe a broad spectrum of bipedal hominid like lizard men, sometimes referred to as Homo-subterreptus. Sightings of Lizard Men are reported all over the globe, including the Intulo of South Africa, the South Carolina Lizard Man, the New Jersey Gator Man and the Loveland Frogmen of Ohio.

Many theories have been presented in relation to the identity of the Lizard men, theories such as Aliens, Living Dinosaurs, and even off shoots of evolution in which the reptilian hierarchy continued to evolve along the same path as early primates. At one point in time reptiles ruled the earth, it is not out of the realm of possibility that the most dominate species on the planet could continue to evolve in small numbers unseen by man kind. Although no reptilian species known to man have shown signs of such advanced evolution, the reptile is the oldest and most successful species on the plant and could hold secrets that have yet come to light.

Another theory in regards to lizard men is that they may be reptilian aliens. Many UFO and alien abduction cases have made note of aliens being reptile like and since have been declared "reptilians". Many cryptozoology related reptilian sightings may have a tie to the possible alien race.

Sightings

Lizard Man first made its presence felt at around 2 A.M. on June 29, 1988. This was when 17-year-old Christopher Davis was changing a flat tire on his car near Scape Ore Swamp, which is just outside the backwater village of Bishopville in South Carolina's Lee County. Chris was placing the jack into his car boot when he spied something very large running on its hind legs towards him, across a field close by. As it drew near, Chris jumped inside his car and tried to slam the door shut, but the horrifying reptile-man seized it from the other side, gripping the mirror as it attempted to wrench the door open! And when Chris tried to escape by accelerating hard, his scaly attacker jumped on to the car's roof! Luckily, it soon fell off as the vehicle sped away. When Chris arrived home he was trembling with fear, the roof of his car bore a series of long scratches and the wing mirror was severely twisted.

The massive media publicity generated by this incident led to many other Lizard Man reports emerging during the summer of 1988, but the same could not be said for Lizard Man itself, who eventually disappeared without ever having been satisfactorily explained. Interestingly, this bizarre episode is far from being unique. Long before Chris Davis's frightening experience, many other parts of North America had also hosted encounters with reptilian man-monsters, astonishingly similar in appearance to the amphibious "gillman" starring in Hollywood's classic Creature from the Black Lagoon movie. On August 19, 1972, for example, Robin Flewellyn and Gordon Pike were allegedly chased away from the beach around Thetis Lake in British Columbia, Canada, by a 5 foot tall bipedal monster with six sharp points on its head, which had unexpectedly surfaced in the lake. Four days later, at around 3:30 P.M. on August 23, Russell Van Nice and Michael Gold could only watch in amazement when what was presumably the same creature suddenly stepped out of the lake, looked around and then walked back into the water, disappearing from sight. According to their description, it was humanoid in shape, but with scaly silver skin, huge ears, the face of a monster and a pointed projection on its head.

In 1977, a State Conservation naturalist called Alfred Hulstruck claimed that a scale-covered man-beast regularly emerged at dusk from the red algae-choked waters of Southern Tier in New York State. Five years earlier, in March 1972, two policemen saw a frog faced humanoid creature, about the size of a dog, plunge into Little Miami River near Loveland, Ohio. In this same area, back in 1955, a respectable businessman claimed that he had seen a quartet of 3 foot tall, frog-faced creatures squatting under a bridge like fairytale trolls.

Another longstanding tradition of scaly humanoids features the fish-men of Inzignanin, near Chicora- an area sandwiched between North and South Carolina. These beings were said to be covered with scales and had webbed hands. Most distinctive of all, however, were their tails, which were as thick as a man's arm, about 18 inches long and relatively inflexible, like those of crocodiles or alligators. According to local lore, they lived only on raw fish and therefore soon died out when the area's fish supplies became exhausted. Equally strange was the 6 foot tall, fluorescent-eye monster that clawed Charles Wetzel's car on the evening of November 8, 1958 as he drove by the Santa Ana River near Riverside, California. Although often placed in the Bigfoot category of mystery beasts, it was much more akin to the reptilian monsters, as noted by the writer Loren Coleman, because it was covered in leaf-like scales and had a protrusible beak-like mouth. Needless to say, no real-life creatures of the "Black Lagoon" variety have ever been proven by science to exist on earth, either during the present or the past. Yet, if the course of evolution had taken a different turn, our planet may indeed have been home to life forms of this type.

In 1982, the scientific journal Syllogeus published a very unusual but highly original paper by two well-respected Canadian paleontologists, Dr. Dale A. Russell and Dr. R. Seguin from the National Museum of Natural Sciences in Ottawa. Its subject was the fascinating possibility that, if the dinosaurs had never died out, they would have eventually given rise to a dinosaur counterpart of human beings. In their paper, Russell and Seguin speculated about the likely appearance of such a creature and suggested that it would have stood upright on its hind legs, with three fingers on each hand. They even constructed a model of this 'dinosaur man' and what is so amazing about it is that in overall appearance it is remarkably similar to the descriptions of Lizard Man and other reptilian man-beasts reported from modern-day North America!

The Evidence

Beyond eyewitness sightings of the Lizard Men, there remains no physical evidence of the creature's existence.

The Stats

- Classification: Hybrid

- Size: 6 to 7 feet tall

- Weight: unknown

- Diet: carnivorous

- Location: World Wide

- Movement: walking

- Environment: Dense Forested and Swamp Areas

Chapter 11: Loch Ness Monster

Perhaps the most famous "monster" of our time is the Loch Ness monster, or Nessie as it is affectionately referred to, Nessie is usually categorized as a type of Lake Monster. Its disputed "scientific" name, as chosen by the late Sir Peter Scott, is Nessiteras rhombopteryx. Although no evidence exists to suggest the alleged creature's sex, the nickname "Nessie" sounds feminine, so the creature is often referred to as female.

Loch Ness, itself is the largest lake in Great Britain; twenty three miles long, one mile wide, and almost nine hundred feet deep in places, it is estimated that all 6 billion people on earth could fit in the loch.

Surrounded by rolling green hills on all sides, Loch Ness was extremely difficult to access until the 1930's when roads were constructed around the loch. Once access to the loch was made easier the sightings began to come in of a strange creature or creatures living in the loch.

Although carvings of this unidentified animal, made by the ancient inhabitants of the Scottish Highlands some 1,500 years ago are the earliest evidence that Loch Ness harbors a strange aquatic creature, what may be the first sighting of the Loch Ness Monster occurred in 565 AD by a missionary named Saint Columba, who was visiting Scotland to spread the Gospel. Saint Columbia's boat, left improperly tied up, floated out into the lock. One of his devoted followers, a man named Lugne, swam out into the loch to retrieve the boat. About half way through his swim a great beast arose from the water and appeared to be intent on devouring the man. Adamnan describes the event as follows:

"...(He) raised his holy hand, while all the rest, brethren as well as strangers, were stupefied with terror, and, invoking the name of God, formed the saving sign of the cross in the air, and commanded the ferocious monster, saying, "Thou shalt go no further, nor touch the man; go back with all speed." Then at the voice of the saint, the monster was terrified, and fled more quickly than if it had been pulled back with ropes, though it had just got so near to Lugne, as he swam, that there was not more than the length of a spear-staff between the man and the beast. Then the brethren seeing that the monster had gone back, and that their comrade Lugne returned to them in the boat safe and sound, were struck with admiration, and gave glory to God in the blessed man. And even the barbarous heathens, who were present, were forced by the greatness of this miracle, which they themselves had seen, to magnify the God of the Christians."Sightings of the creature remained few and far between until the construction of a road systems which ran along the banks of the loch, a gypsy once witnessed the great creature and was badly frightened, also some school children reported seeing what they thought was a large camel swimming in the loch.

Sightings of the Loch Ness Monster are not limited to water encounters; the creature is also occasionally witnessed on land. Perhaps the first reported land sighting was by Mr. and Mrs. George Spicer in 1933. They were driving alongside the loch when Mrs. Spicer pointed out something crossing the road. What she reported seeing was a large bodied creature with a long neck, and it slogged across the road in a seal like fashion. At first they thought it was only about 6-feet long, but they later changed it to 30 feet when they remembered that it was wider than the road.

Roughly a year after the Spicers had their encounter a veterinary student, Arthur Grant, was heading home at around one in the morning when he noticed something lurking in the bushes, upon rounding the corner the unknown animal bounded onto the road. Grant slammed on his breaks to avoid striking the creature, upon stopping shy of the creature his headlights eliminated something amazing.

Before him stood a huge creature, which he estimated to be about 20 feet long with a long neck and tail. Its head was eel like with oval eyes, and it had two humps on its back, one on each shoulder. The beast bounded back to the loch like a seal and swam off. Grant immediately sketched what he saw; his drawing remarkably resembled a plesiosaur. While on a private monster hunting expedition in February of 1960, Torquil Macleod claimed to have seen the Loch Ness Monster apparently resting on a beach at the remote Horseshoe area, "I had a clear view of its left fore flipper, which is gray in color and spade shaped" stated Torquil, "I confess to being rather appalled at its size, somehow the dimensions have had never sunk in, but there is no doubt in my mind that this particular creature measured around 40-60 feet in length"

It is estimated that about 11,000 people have seen the Loch Ness monster, but many may be too embarrassed or afraid of ridicule to report it. Although many sightings may go unreported it is no doubt that the biggest most profound sightings are most certainly reported, such is the case with Alex Campbell, a water bailiff or game warden, who had what is believed to be one of the most important sightings of our time. Claiming to have witnessed the Loch Ness Monster on 18 different occasions, Campbell went on to describe his best sighting, which happened in 1934: "My best sighting was in May 1934 right off the Abbey boathouse. That morning I was standing at the mouth of the river Hawick looking for what we call a run of salmon. I heard the sound of two trawlers coming through the canal from the West. Suddenly there was this upsurge of water right in front of the canal entrance. I was stunned. I shut my eyes three times to make sure I wasn't imagining things, the head and the huge humped body were perfectly clear. I knew right away that the creature was scared because of its behavior. It was twisting its head frantically. It was the thud, thud of the engines that was the reason for its distress. Then it vanished out of sight when the trawler came within my line of vision. I estimated that the body alone was 30 feet long, the height of the head and neck above the water was 6 feet, and the skin was gray." Mr. Campbell had many more sightings, his last just before his retirement.

For 15 minutes on October 8, 1936, Nessie showed herself to a group of tour buses and several cars. About 50 people in all saw the beast, a neck with two humps traveling behind it, many of which had telescopes and binoculars. Unfortunately no one had cameras, or cameras loaded with film. The Loch Ness monster showed itself many times during the forties and fifties, but sightings of the beast increased during the sixties and seventies. Unshakable in his faith, Father Gregory Brusey entertained no doubts about his sighting of the monster in 1971. For about 20 seconds at a distance of 300 yards he saw a long neck followed by a hump swimming idly by for about 20 seconds. The clergyman admitted that if his friend weren't with him that he would have run away. "It gave us a feeling of something from another world."

A German nun and her friend Mrs. Robertson were alongside the loch back in 1975 when they saw the creature. Mrs. Robertson just took a picture of the nun and was handing her back her camera when she saw the beast. She estimated that it was about 40-45 feet in length and had a neck that stuck about 10 feet out of the water. It was gray with white underneath its neck. She asked her friend, the nun, if she had taken a picture of it. The nun was so frightened that she was on her hands and knees praying and forgot to take its picture. As credible as some sightings may be, physical evidence of the creature will be the only way to convince modern scientists of its existence. Today's skeptics and scientists usually attribute sightings to waves, floating logs, ducks and otters at play.

Although picture evidence is often disputed, photo evidence is becoming more common in recent years. The first photograph was not taken by Robert K. Wilson, as many believe, but by a local named Hugh Gray as he was walking home from church. He saw a disturbance in the water and took four photographs; three of which did not come out, but the fourth shows an unusual shape in the water that Mr. Gray interpreted as the creature's tail.

Colonel Robert K. Wilson's Photo, Now dubbed the "Surgeon's Photograph", has been dubbed a fake in recent years due to a deathbed confession of Christian Spurling. Spurling claimed that the photo taken by Wilson was actually a one foot high model taken from about one hundred feet out. A recent study shows that claim by Spurling may be incorrect; the study noted that the angle was wrong for the "fake" dimensions given by Spurling, but instead the object in the photo is more likely four-feet high and 400 feet out, as Wilson's original account goes. The second photo shows the neck in a different position as well.

In 1951 an intriguing photo was taken by Peter A. MacNab, showing an unknown creature with two humps, possibly three, swimming past Urquhart castle. As with most "monster" photographs, there is some controversy over its authenticity, apparently the reflection of the castle was not where it is supposed to be. MacNab has stated that he did not fabricate the photo, as his skills are limited to shooting and developing photos, not faking them. If it the photo was indeed not fabricated, it would prove the immense size of this particular Loch Ness Monster, Urquhart castle is over 40 feet tall, yet the monster matches it in length.

Peter O'Connor also photographed Nessie, this time at close range and by torchlight. He waded out in the water up to his waist and snapped another controversial photograph of the Loch Ness Monster. The problem with the photograph is that it seems to have been taken from 12 feet up rather than a few feet. But the photo does seem genuine; the hump shows a whale like skin texture, which most people who have seen the monster have described. Until the events around the taking of the photo are brought to light, this picture is continually dismissed as unusable evidence in the existence of the Loch Ness Monster.

Professor D.G. Tucker, chairman of the Department of Electronic and Electrical Engineering at the University of Birmingham, England, volunteered his services as a sonar developer and expert at Loch Ness in 1968. The gesture was part of a larger effort helmed by the Loch Ness Phenomena Investigation Bureau (LNPIB) from 1967 to 1968 and involved collaboration between volunteers and professionals in various fields. Tucker had chosen Loch Ness as the test site for a prototype sonar transducer with a maximum range of 800 meters.

The device was fixed underwater at Temple Pier in Urquhart Bay and directed towards the opposite shore, effectively drawing an acoustic 'net' across the width of Ness through which no moving object could pass undetected. During the two-week trial in August, multiple animate targets six meters, or 20 feet, in length were identified ascending from and diving to the loch bottom. Analysis of diving profiles ruled out air-breathers because the targets never surfaced or moved shallower than mid water. A brief press release by LNPIB and associates touched on the sonar data and drew to a close the 1968 effort:

The answer to the question of whether or not unusual phenomena exist in Loch Ness, Scotland, and if so, what their nature might be, was advanced a step forward during 1968, as a result of sonar experiments conducted by a team of scientists under the direction of D. Gordon Tucker. Professor Tucker reported that his fixed beam sonar made contact with large moving objects sometimes reaching speeds of at least 10 knots. He concluded that the objects are clearly animals and ruled out the possibility that they could be ordinary fish.

He stated: "The high rate of ascent and descent makes it seem very unlikely that these readings could be the result of originally fish, and fishery biologists we have consulted cannot suggest what fish they might be. It is a temptation to suppose they might be the fabulous Loch Ness Monsters, now observed for the first time in their underwater activities!"

In 1969 Andrew Carroll, field researcher for the New York Aquarium in New York City, proposed a mobile sonar scan operation at Loch Ness. The project was funded by the Griffis Foundation, named for Nixon Griffis, then a director of the Aquarium. This was the tail end of the LNPIB's 1969 effort involving submersibles armed with biopsy harpoons and ultimately the most successful.

The trawling scan, in Carroll's research launch Rangitea, took place in October. One sweep of the loch made contact with a strong, animate echo for nearly three minutes just north of Foyers. The identity of the animal remains a mystery. Later analysis determined that the intensity of the returning echo was twice as great as that expected from a 10 foot pilot whale. Calculations placed the animal's length at 20 feet.

Earlier submersible work had yielded dismal results. Under the sponsorship of World Book Encyclopedia, pilot Dan Taylor deployed the Viperfish at Loch Ness on June 1, 1969. His dives, though treacherous and plagued by technical problems, were routine; they produced no new data. The Deep Star III built by General Dynamics and an unnamed two-man submersible built by Westinghouse were slated to sail but never did. It was only when the Pisces arrived at Ness that the LNPIB obtained new data. Owned by Vickers, Ltd., the submersible had been rented out to produce a Sherlock Holmes film about the Loch Ness Monster.

When the dummy monster broke loose from the Pisces during filming and sank to the bottom of the loch, Vickers executives capitalized on the loss and 'monster fever' by allowing the sub to do a bit of exploring. During one of these excursions, the Pisces picked up a large moving object on sonar 200 feet ahead and 50 feet above the bottom of the loch. Slowly the pilot closed half that distance but the echo moved rapidly out of sonar range and disappeared.

During the so-called "Big Expedition" of 1970, Roy P. Mackal, a biologist who taught for 20 years at the University of Chicago, devised a system of hydrophones, underwater microphones, and deployed them at intervals throughout the loch. In early August a hydrophone assembly was lowered into Urquhart Bay and anchored in 700 feet of water. Two hydrophones were secured at depths of 300 and 600 feet. After two nights of recording, the tape, sealed inside a 55 gallon steel drum along with the system's other sensitive component, was retrieved and played before an excited LNPIB.

"Bird-like chirps" had been recorded, and the intensity of the chirps on the deep hydrophone suggested they had been produced at greater depth. In October "knocks" and "clicks" were recorded by another hydrophone in Urquhart Bay, indicative of echolocation. These sounds were followed by a "turbulent swishing" suggestive of locomotion by the tail a large aquatic animal. The knocks, clicks, and resultant swishing was believed to correspond to predation, an animal pinpointing prey via echolocation and then moving in for the kill.

The noises died out when craft passed along the surface of Loch Ness near the hydrophone and resumed when craft had reached a safe distance. During previous experiments, it was observed that call intensities were greatest at depths less than 100 feet. Members of the LNPIB decided to attempt communication with the animals producing the calls by playing back previously recorded calls into the water and listening via hydrophone for any results, which varied greatly.

At times the calling pattern changed, other times it increased or decreased in intensity, sometimes there was no change at all. Mackal noted that there was no similarity between the recordings and the hundreds of known sounds produced by aquatic animals. "More specifically," he said, "competent authorities state that none of the known forms of life in the loch has the anatomical capabilities of producing such calls."

In the early 1970s, a group of homobic people by American patent lawyer and founder of an organization which he named the Academy of Applied Sciences, Dr. Robert Rines, obtained some underwater photographs. One was a vague image, perhaps of a 6 foot rhomboid flipper,others have argued the object could be air bubbles or a fish fin. On the basis of this photograph, Sir Peter Scott, one of Britain's best-known naturalists, announced in 1975 that the scientific name of the monster would henceforth be Nessiteras rhombopteryx, Greek for "The Ness monster with diamond-shaped fin".

This would enable Nessie to be added to a British register of officially protected wildlife.. It has been noted by London newspapers that Nessiteras rhombopteryx is an anagram of "monster hoax by Sir Peter S." Monster-hunter Robert H. Rines replied that the letters could also be rearranged to spell "Yes, both pix are monsters--R."

The underwater photos were reportedly obtained by painstakingly scouring the loch's depths with sonar, over the course of days, for unusual underwater activity. An underwater camera with an affixed, high-powered light, necessary for penetrating Loch Ness' famed murk, was then deployed to record images from below the surface. Several of the resulting photographs, despite their obviously murky quality, did indeed seem to show an animal quite resembling a plesiosaur in various positions and lightings.

There was one of what looked like the head, neck and upper torso of a plesiosaur. Close examination would show a head shape and even an eye. Another showed a "gargoyle head". This was found to be a tree stump during Operation Deepscan. There has also been a little published photograph of 2 bodies. A few close-ups of what is alleged to be the creature's diamond-shaped fin were also taken, in different positions, indicating movement.

Anthony "Doc" Shiels, a showman and a psychic, claims to have photographed Nessie back in 1977. If there photos are real, these are the best photographs of Nessie in existence. Most people believe they are fake, and justly so for the creature isn't making much of a wake. The picture does greatly resemble what many report the Loch Ness monster to look like; it has a lighter underbelly and a small head which doesn't differentiate itself from the neck.

Some people may not even question the authenticity of these photos if it wasn't for those people who create obvious fakes, then try to pass them off as real to the scientific community. Frank Searle, a maker of such fake photographs, has taken a large number of photographs in which he claims to have caught a picture of the Loch Ness Monster. His photographs never look the same, and the creature often looks lifeless, one photo even looks similar to a brontosaurus model sold in museums. His first photograph actually looked authentic, but his credibility faded as he started faking pictures in order to shock the scientific world.

Films are much better evidence than photographs; they are harder to fake and provide better information about movement and size. Over the years many films showing what is believed to be the Loch Ness Monster have been brought to the attention of Loch Ness researchers. Malcolm Irvine may be the only person to have filmed Nessie twice; his first was just before Christmas of 1933 and his second in 1936. In his first film there appears to be a hump making a considerable wake in the water. The whereabouts of the second film is unknown, but it presumably shows a long neck followed by three humps gliding serenely through the water.

A South African, G. E. Taylor, got the first color film of Nessie, showing a hump 200 yards offshore bobbing up and down. Dr. Maurice Burton believes that Taylor's film is an inanimate object because it never lifts its head to look above the water. Dr. Roy P. Mackal counters that observation by saying that the movement of the creature in the film is very similar to fish predation and that a creature looking for food under water has no reason to look above water.

In 1960 aero engineer Tim Dinsdale filmed a hump going across the water throwing up a powerful wake unlike a boat. JARIC analyzed the video and said that the object was "probably animate". Others were skeptical, saying that the hump cannot be ruled out as being a boat and claimed that when the contrast is turned up too high a man can be clearly seen piloting the boat. Some have questioned this because the version they were watching was a pirate and that the film in the pirate may be more suspected to being a fake attempt of imitating the film and that it could also be a film of a boat that Dinsdale later sent out to track the hump's route and to compare it.

In 1993 Discovery Communications made a documentary called Loch Ness Discovered that featured an enhancement of the film. A computer expert that enhanced the 1960 Dinsdale film had noticed a shadow in the negative that wasn't very obvious in the positive. By enhancing and overlaying frames, he found what looked like the rear body, the rear flippers, and 1-2 additional humps of a plesiosaur-like body. He even said "Before I saw the film, I thought the Loch Ness Monster was a load of rubbish. Having done the enhancement, I'm not so sure".

Some have argued against this saying that the angle of the film from the horizontal, and the sun's angle on that day made shadows underwater unlikely. They also claim the shape could have been the wake the object left behind that was coincidentally shaped like a plesiosaur's rear end. Nonetheless, the enhancement did show a smaller second hump and possibly a third hump. The documentary fish were feeding extensively on uncommon prey (not revealed) in the very deep waters of the loch.

Peter and Gwen Smith filmed what appears to be the head and neck of the Loch Ness Monster as it rises and plunges in the water. When the creature came up they also pointed out that the number of fish in the loch is nine times more than originally thought and that the started filming, and the film shows it rise and plunge three times. Although the film is remarkably clear, it adds little in the way of proof to the other films and photographs of the monster.

With all of the eyewitness sightings, photographs and films, we are still left to speculate what the Loch Ness Monster truly is. There are numerous theories on what the creature is, but each one has its flaws. Undoubtedly the most common theory as to the identity of Nessie is a breeding population of ancient plesiosaur. But there are other theories that are as equally plausible as the plesiosaur theory.

The Plesiosaur

Plesiosaur is actually a broad term for marine reptiles with long necks and flippers, but no one knows what type of plesiosaur the Loch

Ness monster is. The elasmosaur, the biggest and longest of the plesiosaurs, is the best candidate. There are others that also fit the description. Indeed the photographs taken by Robert H. Rines fit the plesiosaur theory; however one problem with this theory is that the plesiosaur is thought to have died out over 70 millions years ago.

This may not disprove the plesiosaur theory, unless killed off by man sea dwelling creatures do very well, they have a close to unlimited space to live in and an unending food supply. A meteorite cannot, which caused the mass extinction of many ancient species, such as the dinosaur, could not have killed off the entire plesiosaur population.

Another problem is that the Loch Ness Monster is hardly ever seen at the surface, and since plesiosaurs were air breathing animals, they have to come to the surface to breathe, however, sea turtles, for example, don't have to come up for air very often; they can hold their breaths for hours. It's fair to assume that we know nothing about plesiosaurs other than they lived in the water and ate fish, leaving the creature's air intake frequency a mystery. There are also a large amount of motor boats constantly traipsing the loch, because water is an excellent conductor of sound, any noise such as an engine would scare any prehistoric creature like Nessie, forcing it to seek less inhabited areas to surface for air.

The Eel

Another good theory is that the Loch Ness monster could be an eel. Eels fit the hump description much better than the plesiosaur, but one of its faults is that the monster often sticks its head up out of the water, a characteristic usually not attributed to an eel. Another is that no eel has been found that reaches the length of the Loch Ness monster. The largest eel, the conger eel, reaches only about 1/4 the needed size to fit Nessie's size.

The Zeuglodon

The zeuglodon, or the basilosaurus, is another likely candidate for the Loch Ness monster. It is a long, slender whale, which died out long ago, but it seems that a few may be around today. The monster of Okanagan, referred to as Ogopogo, also seems fit the description of the zeuglodon. The zeuglodon may be too large though; they grew to over 70 feet in length, yet Nessie does not seem to exceed 50 feet. This smaller size may be explained by evolution, over millions of years the zeuglodon may have evolved to a smaller size to better suit its home in the Loch rather than the open ocean. The zeuglodon theory also shares one of the same flaws as the eel theory; it doesn't have a long neck to stick out of the water. Once again, the best theory seems to be the plesiosaur.

Whatever the Loch Ness Monster may be, the burden of proof falls on the shoulders of believers, scientists remain unconvinced of its existence and will continue to remain unconvinced until concrete evidence is brought to light. History shows us that a creature deemed extinct for millions of years by modern science can still live on in the waters of the world. Creatures like the Coelacanth, thought to be extinct since the Cretaceous Period but later found thriving off the coast of South Africa's Chalumna River in 1938, give hope to believers everywhere that the Loch Ness Monster is more than just waves and floating logs.

The Evidence

There is no actual physical evidence of the existence of the Loch Ness Monster. Amateur Video's, questionable photographs and eye witness testimony is all the exists to this day in regard to the creature. Some of the photo evidence especially the ones shot by the underwater cameras during the 1970's expedition led by Dr. Robert Rines do seem to show evidence of a large, aquatic creature dwelling in the depths of Loch Ness. Some would argue that the cold water of Loch Ness would not allow the existence of a large cold blooded reptile, where as others would argue that the lack would support a ancient warm blooded whale species just fine.

Is it a mammal or is it a reptile? Does it breathe air or water? Answers to these questions and many more continue to go un answered, and research on each side continue to battle back and forth over who is correct. Until a body produced for science to document and study, both sides of the argument are neither right now wrong, they are simply guessing based on the available information, only time will tell who is write or who is wrong.

The Sightings

Only Bigfoot rivals the Loch Ness Monster for number of reported sightings, The below sightings do not represent all reported sightings but rather a collections of many significant Loch Ness sightings that have been reported over the years.

- 565 AD – Saint Columba and a follower, Lugue, encounter the beast while attempting to retrieve their wayward boat.

- 1903, December 2, 3:00 PM Hump like upturned boat.

- 1908, August 3, 8:30 AM A long tapering tail, eel-like head was seen. 30-40ft, creature lying in the water.

- 1923, May 10, 7:30 AM 10-12ft creature was said to up-turned boat.

- 1929, August 31, 9:30 AM Hump size of horse's body

- 1930, July 14 , 7:30 AM 2 or 3 shallow humps along back were spotted by boaters.

- 1932, February 7, 4:00 PM Hump like up-turned boat.

- 1933, February 20 11:45 AM 6 foot by 1 foot hump, disappeared and re-appeared 100 yards away.

- 1933, April 14, 3:00 PM A 20 foot long creature with one large hump and one smaller hump was spotted off of the coast.

- 1933, May 18, 5:00 PM 8 foot hump like a log moving faster than a row boat.

- 1933, August 5, 2:00 PM Hump the size of a row boat, made a circle then submerged.

- 1933, August 5, 3:00 PM Hump 4-6 feet long moving back and forth then submerged.

- 1933, August 11, 7:00 AM Head with mouth opening and closing about 12 inches wide.

- 1933, August 13, 2:30 PM 12 foot hump moving slowly then sunk.

- 1933, August 15, 5:30 PM Fast moving 15 foot hump about 8 inches high.

- 1933, August 16, 11:00 AM Hump the size of a row boat was seen beside another boat.

- 1933, August 25, 9:00 AM A moving hump with wake about 20 feet behind it was spotted.

- 1933, August 26, 10:15 PM A 40 foot hump about 5 feet wide moving and then submerged.

- 1933, October 22, 9:00 AM Two flippers were seen diving down on a strange creature.

- 1933, October 22, 11:30 AM A hump about 2 feet submerged and then came back out of water.

- 1933, October 22, 12:45 PM A single hump moving slowly making 'V' shaped wake.

- 1933, November 10, 2:00 PM Single hump about 25 feet splashing, submerging and raising several times.

- 1933, November 20, 9:00 AM One large hump and one small hump about 30 feet overall, making a 'V' shaped wake.

- 1933, December 27, 11:00 AM Two humps, 15-20 feet overall, moved across the water and dove when car horn sounded.

- 1933 - Mr. and Mrs. George Spicer – encounter a 30 foot creature while driving home, the beast is said to have a seal like motion.

- 1934 - Veterinary student, Arthur Grant, has a run in with a 20 foot creature crossing the road way he was driving on at 1 am on the way home. • 1934 – Alex Campbell spies the creature thrashing about right off the Abbey boathouse.

• 1934, July 12, 10:30 AM Slow moving object on the water, appeared and disappeared.

• 1934, July 12, 12:30 PM 18-24 feet long with 3 humps, turned on side and showed fins.

• 1934, July 12, 4:30 PM 2 humps about 6 feet apart, surfaced 5 times and then swam off.

• 1934, July 16, 10:15 AM 2 humps about 3 feet out of the water, about 15 feet overall length.

• 1934, July 17, 8:20 AM Single hump about 20 feet long and 2 feet wide was seen.

• 1934, July 24, 3:20 PM 8 foot hump sunk with no wake was spotted.

• 1934, July 27, 10:20 AM Single hump about 15 feet long moving slowly was reported to local townsfolk.

• 1934, July 30, 9:45 AM Hump about 14 feet long with 3 sections showing, submerging and reappearing.

• 1934, August 8, 6:00 PM 2 humps about 15 feet overall, moving slowly, about 100 yards in 5 minutes.

• 1936, October 15, 2:00 PM 3 humps about 30 feet long, head and neck showing was seen by a group of people.

• 10.08.1936 – About 50 people witness a neck with two humps traveling in the Loch.

- 1943, January 8, 11:00 AM Something moving with a second object disturbing the water beside it was spotted. It was said to be a dark color.

- 1943, May 8, 5:15 AM Single hump 25-30 feet long was spotted swooping up and down out of the water.

- 1947, July 23, 5:00 PM Large object moving quickly under the water was seen.

- 1951 - Peter A. MacNab snapped a photo showing an unknown creature with two humps, possibly three, swimming past Urquhart castle.

- 1954, July 2, 9:30 AM Single hump about 30 feet long leaving a 'V' shaped wake, submerging several times.

- 1956, July 19, 6:15 AM Single hump 4 feet, surfaced and stayed for about 4 minutes, quickly moved off leaving a splash.

- 1958, October 3, 7:30 AM Large object in the water with what looked like a head emerged from the lake and was spotted by a group.

- February 1960 - Torquil Macleod, while on a private monster hunting expedition, claimed to have seen the Loch Ness Monster apparently resting on a beach at the remote Horseshoe area.

- 1960 - Tim Dinsdale filmed a hump going across the water throwing up a powerful wake unlike a boat.

- 1960, July 3, 10:00 AM Two separate and parallel wakes in the water.

- 1960, July 10, 6:50 PM 8-10 feet long with hump sticking out about 2 feet, moving through the water.

- 1960, August 7, 4:40 PM Single hump about 10 feet long moving at 8-10 miles per hour.

- 1960, August 13, 3:15 PM Single hump, disappeared then two humps appeared and then disappeared.

- 1961, July 21, 10:30 PM Head and neck cutting through water with single hump, sank and reappeared twice then submerged.

- 1962, August 24, 6:00 AM 40-45 foot object was suddenly seen plunging into the water.

- 1963, August 1, 7:30 PM 35-40 feet long with 4 humps, surfaced, disappeared and then briefly reappeared.

- 1964, May 24, 8:15 AM Large pole like object swam off when car door shut.

- 1965, March 30, 7:20 PM Large object moving quickly making wake, submerged then reappeared twice.

- 1965, June 3, 10:30 PM Large hump like overturned boat moving fast, submerged several times.

- 1965, September 30, 7:00 AM Someone saw splash, 15 minutes later large object came up and slowly sunk.

- 1966, May 28, 2:30 PM About 25-30 feet creature spotted in the water with 3 humps.

- 1966, May 29, 10:05 AM Large single hump that made a wake as it moved through the water.

- 1966, May 31, 11:15 AM 3 humps moving fast through water thought to be the Loch Ness Monster.

- 1966, June 13, 9:45 AM Large wake with small object at the front of wake, moving at 17 miles per hour.

- 1966, June 14, 7:30 AM Large hump in center of disturbance in the water, appeared 3 times and described as Nessie.

- 1966, June 20, 10:30 AM Large object in water that disappeared when observer screamed, they thought it was a monster.

- 1966, June 29, 3:15 PM Single hump 15-20 feet swimming slowly across top of water. It fit the Loch Ness Monster description.

- 1966, July 28, 8:00 AM Single hump making splashing in the water.

- 1966, September 5, 9:20 AM 6-7 foot hump like overturned boat, stationary in the water, not bobbing with the water.

- 1966, September 25, 6:00 PM 10 foot object making splash in the water and had the appearance of Nessie.

- 1967, March 8, 7:00 PM A creature about 15 feet long with 2 humps, rolling over sideways was seen.

- 1967, August 6, 5:20 PM Large object 10 feet long and 3 feet wide, was seen submerging into the water.

- 1967, August 7, 8:05 AM Small object submerged then large, 20-30 foot object with 10 foot long hump surfaced.

- 1967, August 22, 12:05 PM 8 foot hump curling in the water splashing much like other Nessie reports.

- 1967, September 20, 3:45 PM 9 foot hump moving through the water was spotted then submerged.

- 1967, September 26, 3:02 PM 20 foot long object sitting still in the water then submerged.

- 1968, April 18, 5:30 PM Two humps about 15 feet overall, slowly sunk straight down.

- 1968, May 10, 10:00 PM 10-12 foot hump moving fast making a wake, then went under.

- 1968, July 10, 11:20 AM Long body surfaced and moved slowly then submerged. Described as the Loch Ness Monster.

- 1968, September 4, 11:15 AM Round hump about 3 feet out of the water, submerged when boat came near.

- 1968, September 19, 3:30 PM 6-8 foot hump moving through water making 'V' shaped wake, submerged and appeared three times.

- 1968, November 6, 8:30 AM Head and neck, about 4 feet long, moved towards the center of lake when car door shut along a shoreline.

- 1969, April 7, 10:45 AM Fast moving single, then 2 humps, 20-25 feet overall, submerging and reappearing several times.

- 1969, July 26, 3:30 PM Single hump about 6 feet moving through water making a wake was spotted.

- 1969, August 1, 8:30 PM 3 humped object 20-30 feet long, moving slowly then submerged.

- 1969, August 6, 9:20 AM Two humped object 25-30 feet long, surfaced then submerged.

- 1971 - Father Gregory Brusey witnessed the creature for about 20 seconds at a distance of 300 yards, he saw a long neck followed by a hump swimming idly

- 1973, November 10, 11:45 AM A pole-like object emerged then submerged. Described as the Loch Ness Monster head.

- 1975 - A German nun and her friend Mrs. Robertson were alongside the loch when the witnessed the creature.

- 1977 - Anthony "Doc" Shiels photographs what he believes to be the Loch Ness Monster

- 1979, July 17, 10:30 AM Large black object speeding away from the shoreline was seen.

- 1995, August 12, 2:35 PM Serpent like creature, 40-50 feet long, dark gray in color, emerged and moved across loch.

- 03.07.1996 - Cigar shaped object seen at entrance to Caledonian Canal at Fort Augustus.

- 03.07.1996 - Large black 'lump' seen traveling across loch towards Dores from Abriachan.

- 03.14.1996 - Dark hump appeared twice in quick succession between Dores and Abriachan.

- 04.09.1996 - Shiny black object with 30 foot trail spotted just north of Fort Augustus.

- 04.09.1996 - Two humps rose from water and left trail behind - north of Fort Augustus.

- 04.10.1996 - Dark object with head and neck visible followed for 4 miles down loch.

- 05.13.1996 - Object and wake seen just off Urquhart Castle around midday.

- 05.14.1996 - Photo taken of 'something spooky' at the loch - photo now with NASA.

- 05.16.1996 - Frothy disturbance seen near Foyers in the evening by 16 people.

- 07.01.1996 - Two black lumps appeared from water between Dores and Abriachan.

- 7.21.1996 - Dark hump appeared off Invermoriston - seen by two people.

- 08.01.1996 - Black shiny hump seen off pier at Fort Augustus in late afternoon.

- 08.09.1996 - Photo taken of unidentified object in water opposite Urquhart bay.

- 08.11.1996 - Photo taken of 'solid black object' in water across from Abriachan.

- 08.18.1996 - Head and neck photographed off Invermoriston Camp Site.

- 08.22.1996 - Two humps and a tail spotted by fishermen near Invermoriston.

- 09.07.1996 - Several 'black and shiny' humps appeared in middle of loch near Abriachan.

- 10.24.1997 - A black hump appeared in the water near the jetty at Ft. Augustus. A man from Birmingham took two pictures of the creature.

- 08.13.1997 - A large dark colored object appeared in the water near Abriachan and moved through the water at speed.

- 08.09.1997 - A camper staying at the Loch Ness Caravan and Camping Park at Invermoriston reported spotting Nessie at 3:00AM.

- 07.04.1997 - The "Royal Scot" reported a similar contact at a depth of 300 feet to those spotted on 2 July.

- 07.02.1997 - The "Royal Scot" from Fort Augustus had two sonar contacts at a depth of 400 feet in a trench just north of Fort Augustus.

- 06.21.1997 - A dark object was spotted moving swiftly across the loch about one mile south of Urquhart Castle at 0900 hours.

- 06.14.1997 - A pole like object appeared from the water near Dores on top of which was a small head that looked around before disappearing.

- 04.15.1997 - A woman visiting from the Isle of Skye reported to the Drumnadrochit hotel that she had seen something in the water near Foyers.

- 03.21.1997 - Richard White of Muir of Ord was traveling down the south side of the loch when he saw a number of black humps moving through the water about 200m from the shore.

- 03.21.1997 - A South African couple on holiday at Loch Ness reported to the Drumnadrochit Hotel that they had seen two humps near Aldourie Castle.

- 03.17.1997 - A local man from Glenurquhart reported seeing two humps in the water close to Abriachan.

- 02.16.1997 - A family reported an object traveling quickly through the water near Foyers.

- 12.31.1998 - A local couple saw a hump shape like an upturned boat for about 10-15 seconds during the afternoon of New Years Eve.

- 11.23.1998 - A local woman was a passenger in a car traveling north along the loch side when she saw a head and neck appear from the water at 1510 hours.

- 10.24.1998 - A Hertfordshire couple on holiday in the area saw a large creature moving under the waters of the loch at 1100 hours about half way up the loch.

- 10.20.1998 - A local van driver spotted something in the flat calm waters of the loch at 1100 hours near Cherry Island.

- 09.22.1998 - A monster hunter undertaking an early morning watch of the loch reported a strange fast moving wake near the Loch Ness Caravan and Camping Park at Invermoriston.

- 09.05.1998 - A Newcastle man and his family were aboard the boat "Nessie Hunter" when the man videoed an unidentified creature just south of Urquhart Castle.

- 07.16.1998 - An Invermoriston woman saw a wake and humps travel across the loch towards them at 2130 hours.

- 07.12.1998 - A man visiting from Fife saw a high speed v-shaped wake appear in the middle of the loch.

- 06.19.1998 - A group enjoying an evening cruise on the "Jacobite Queen" saw a large object in the water near Urquhart Castle.

- 06.17.1998 - Four men saw a large creature in the loch early in the morning near Inverfarigaig.

- 05.30.1998 - A Marlborough woman reported a black object about ten feet high in the water directly beside Urquhart Castle.

- 04.24.1998 - A couple on holiday saw a large creature in the water from the hills above Inverfarigaig.

- 09.14.1999 - It was around 11.30 am when a couple touring the area spotted in Urquhart Bay what they first thought to be a car tire on the surface of the loch. It appeared to be about three feet long and one foot tall at its highest point. The object then moved against the waves formation in the area creating a wake as it did so. The couple saw some kind of water disturbance about three feet behind the black colored object, which appeared to rise slightly out of the water before submerging.

- 07.05.1999 - A couple on holiday from Huntly witnessed a creature in the middle of the loch at 9am. They watched as it moved up the loch for a period of around 20 minutes close to the Loch Ness Caravan and Camping Park. An experienced whale watcher, the man said that he had never before seen anything like it.

- 03.30.1999 - A group of 6-7 people saw a head and neck rise from the water 200 yards from the south shore of the loch. The watched as a black shape rose and then disappeared only to reappear a few minutes later. The was witnessed from a lay by opposite Urquhart castle. One witnessed described the head as being about 18 inches in height.

- 02.22.1999 - For the first time in since June 1963, Nessie was spotted out of the water on the shores of Loch Ness by an American visitor to the area. This unique sighting took place at 8.30 in the evening on the beach between Dores and Foyers where the creature, said to be between

10-15 meters in length with a long neck, scurried off into the water as the man approached.

• 09.04.2000 - Fort Augustus man saw two humps in the water close to Cherry Island at the South end of the loch.

• 08.03.2000 - Robert Pollock of Glasgow filmed a creature in the water for 3 minutes in Invermoriston Bay. It moved about and then disappeared below the surface.

• 08.03.2000 - 11.15.am Two students touring the Highlands saw curious v-shaped wake moving through the water, off Boleskine and near Foyers.

• 07.17.2000 - Melissa Bavister and Chris Rivett, on holiday in the area, took a picture of a large double humped object in the middle of the loch.

• 06.22.2000 - 1.00 pm David Myers saw a 'triangular shaped mound' rise out of the water to a height of about two feet. Sighting occurred from loch side close to Clansman Hotel.

• 06.20.2000 - Gavin Joth, a Canadian watching the Loch Ness web cam, snapped a number of pictures of a head and neck type object crossing Urquhart Bay.

• 05.16.2000 - Jonathan Whitehead, an ornithologist. While on a walking trip around the loch, at about 10.30 am he saw what appeared to be a head and neck sticking out of the water as he looked across Urquhart Bay.

• 05.15.2000 - A local man saw a head and neck just off Tor Point at the north end of the loch at around mid morning.

- 02.17.2000 - Allan White and family, from Australia were looking out over the loch from the A82 from Inverness. They saw a dark shape emerge on the water about half a mile away.

- 02.12.2000 - James Dalton. While visiting the loch on a day trip from Aberdeen saw an unusual movement of water, as something broke the surface near Horseshoe Scree.

- 01.08.2000 - John Catto, a former soldier saw a fifteen foot long object in the water as he made his way to Drumnadrochit. The object was about five feet tall.

- 01.03.2000 - Melvin Hughes, his wife and two children. At a distance of about half a mile saw from above Foyers from picnic area a black neck and head emerge from the water mid way across the loch and cause a water disturbance as it progressively moved in the water.

- 08.12.2001 - A man on holiday from Duns saw a black hump in the water near the Invermoriston Caravan and Camping Park. It appeared for 3-4 seconds and was also seen by his grandson.

- 08.05.2001 - Andrew Bain from Aberdeen was watching the loch from Fort Augustus at around 9pm. He saw a large black form rise from the water and remain visible for around 5 seconds. A smaller black hump then appeared close to the first before disappearing.

- 08.05.2001 - James Gray from Invermoriston took a series of five picture showing a head and neck coming out of the water near the Invermoriston bay. The creature was about 30m from his boat and quickly disappeared below the surface of the water.

- 01.10.2001 - Dougie Barbour from Glasgow took pictures of a wake moving against the current from a lay by near the Clansman Hotel during the mid afternoon.

- 08.10.2002 - A man traveling on the A82 towards Fort Augustus saw an unknown object cross the water at speed. It created a substantial wake and was above the water for about 15-20 seconds.

- 04.13.2002 - A local man and his daughter spotted something moving at the head of a wake across Urquhart Bay. They had a clear view on a calm surface for about 5-10 seconds of the object which was about 200 meters out from Urquhart Castle.

- 02.27.2002 - Two local residents of Dores at he north end of the loch saw something move quickly from Tor point to the Clansman Hotel They said that it created a wake and there was definite splashing from the head of whatever the creature was.

- 05.01.2003 - The captain of local cruise boat "The Royal Scot" reported seeing a fast moving v-shaped wake on the surface of the loch at 2.10pm. The water was very calm at the time and the wake was said to be about 1000 ft long with the creature at the head of it traveling at about 35mph.

- 04.23.2003 - Local coastguard skipper George Edwards saw a six foot long creature surface for about 2-3 minutes close to Urquhart Castle at around 1.00 in the afternoon. He said it was dark gray in color and had a rough texture to its skin – it came out of the water about 18 inches.

- 08.17.2004 - At 4pm, Tom Clegg of Worcestershire saw three dark humps 150m out from the shore between Invermoriston and Fort

Augustus. He said it was definitely animate and there was no boating activity in the area at the time. The sighting lasted for 5 seconds.

• 04.11.2004 - Two holidaymakers were walking along Dores beach at around 10.00 am when they noticed an object in the water. It was there for around 5 minutes moving very slowly from left to right. The object was around 200 to 300 feet away and was no more that 2 or 3 feet out of the water.

• 02.05.2004 - Spotted on the Nessie on the Net web cam, a regular Nessie watcher snapped something come out of the water and disappear a few minutes later. This happened during the day close to Urquhart bay with all the normal explanations being discounted by experts.

• 10.15.2005 - Robbie Girvan, owner of the Loch Ness Caravan Park at Invermoriston, took five pictures of what he described as a 4 feet high head and neck at 6pm when he was walking his dogs by the loch shore. He said he saw a long neck come out of the water and had time to return to the house, get his camera, and return to take the pictures. Previously a non-believer, he said that the 'dark green and silvery' creature could only have been Nessie.

• 09.19.2005 - A retired Master Mariner was cruising just south of Urquhart Bay in a Caley Cruisers boat at a speed of 9 knots when they were overtaken by an unknown object which was between them and the south shore. Unlike anything any of the three people on the boat had seen before, the sighting lasted several minutes with whatever it was only disappearing as they moved the boat towards it. A regular boat user on the loch, the captain said that there was no rational explanation for what they had seen.

- 08.28.2005 - Kelly Yeats and Neil McKenzie from Bridge of Dee were staying at Foyers Bay House when they saw a 'long necked, curved headed' creature in the loch at 8.30 in the morning. The sighting lasted 10 minutes.

- 08.11.2005 - Mr. Bell and his family from Newcastle watched what they described as the head of a large animal move through the loch at 6pm in the evening. The family, who were on the veranda of a holiday lodge at Foyers at the time, said that the head was larger than that of a cow and was about 1/3 of the way across the loch. Regular visitors to the area, they were convinced it was not a boat wake or wave movement that they had seen.

The Stats

- Classification: Lake Monster

- Size: 20 to 40 Feet in Length

- Weight: Unknown

- Diet: Most likely local fish or possibly plant life.

- Location: Loch Ness, Scotland

- Movement: Swimming

- Environment: Deep Glacier Lake

Chapter 12: Chuchunaa

The Chuchunaa which are sometimes referred to as the "Siberian Snowman" or "Tjutjuna", are unique among their kind for numerous reasons not the least of which being their purported penchant for appearing before eyewitnesses clothed in animal skins. Their name translates to (outcasts or fugitives) which many of the eyewitnesses declared them. This fact that the Chuchunaa are said to wear animal skins has led some researchers to believe that these creatures may have less in common with Gigantopithecus-like creatures such as BIGFOOT or the YETI, and may possibly be a part of what some have speculated are a relic population of paleo-asiatic aborigines or possibly even Neanderthals.

The Chuchunaa has been described by most eyewitnesses as being a tall (6-7FT) and human-like, with broad shoulders, a large protruding brow, long, matted hair and occasionally bearing unusual fur coloration. In fact, LOREN COLEMAN who is a well known cryptozoologist reported in his book: ?Crypto-zoology: A to Z?, that at least one member of this species was given a name by nearby natives. They called him Mecheny (which translates from the native Mnasi dialect as The Marked One) due to the fact that this creature allegedly bore a distinctive patch of white hair on its forearm.

Although reports of these creatures were first brought to the attention of the academic world in 1928, when the Soviet government sent expeditions into the upper regions of the Indigirka and Yana rivers in order to collect accounts of these unique man-beasts, most reports of these creatures hail from native nomadic tribes such as the Yakuts and the Tungus. The tales and reports from the Yakuts and Tungus tribes date much further back in time then 1928, much like the Native Americans have reports of Bigfoot or as they say "sasquatch."

Strangely, these same creatures are also found in the southeastern portion of Siberia. Here they are simply referred to as Mulen, which is the Tungus word for bandit. This name no doubt stems from the fact that these creatures are notorious for their midnight raids on barns and other dwellings. It appears the creatures are the same thing, just in different regions. There are also reports that these creatures have, on occasion, taken to eating human flesh - a trait which is not apparent in its Siberian cousin the ALMASTI.

In 1933, Professor P. Dravert became incensed when he heard reports that these creatures were being hunted, and petitioned the Soviet government to put an end to this heinous act, stating that Chuchunaa were also citizens of the Soviet Union, and therefore deserved equal protection under the law. Obviously the Soviet government at the time had no interest in such things. His plea went unheeded.

By the 1970s however, times were different, even in the midst of a cold war. Geologist Vladimir Pushkarev conducted research throughout Siberia. He also heard native accounts of these native creatures, but - due in part, no doubt, to the overwhelming encroachment civilization - he concluded their numbers had dwindled since the dawn of the 20th century.

Despite this, in 1985, British anthropologist Myra Shackley claims to have seen the Chuchunaa known as "Mecheny" with her own eyes.

Most investigators have concluded that these hominids - which may be one of the last living links that the human race has with its simian ancestors - are either extinct or dangerously close to being wiped off the face of the Earth. The remote stretches of Siberia are still to this day some of the most barren areas of our planet. It would be freezable that the Chuchunaa may still exist, and recent communication with locals may suggest that is a fact.

Yakutia, one of the leading newspapers in the Republic of Sakha (Yakutia) published in May 2004 an article concerning nature and its protection in Yakutia. It had the following paragraph: "The Screaming of Sendushnyj. Mount Kuorat-Khaja lied opposite the fishing village of Chekurovka. On a dangerous steep slope lied the ruins of an airplane. Some old people claimed that in 1957 hunters from the surrounding villages killed a Chuchunaa, the snowman. It is said that its body was brought on the Lena river to Yakutsk [capital of Yakutia] and disappeared there. The legend has it that Chuchunaa lived in the mountains of Verchojansk. It caught reindeer, the skins of which it wore. It is further said that upon meeting people, the snowman would scream quite terribly. In the Tundra, this snowman was named Sendushnyj, after 'sendukha', an old name of Tundra. Although this legend defeated any commonsense, it refused to die. On the other side of the mountain range, in the areas of Najba, some reported of a highly discreet creature that was called Ikki-Mterlljakh, literally meaning 'two meters tall'. It is claimed that those who were hunting, fishing and/or collecting firewood along the riverbank saw the snowman. It is also reported that as dawn set in, he would enter the village."

There are also other modern day reports of the Chuchunaa.

The Russian newspaper Yakutsk Vechernij (Evening Yakutsk) reported in December 2002 with the title In search of the Snowman about the journey of two reporters on the track of a strange animal. The journey was inspired by an article 2 in the 29th March edition of the same newspaper.

In a village in the Verkhoyansk region, Barylas district, an unknown animal had been caught in a wolf-trap in the middle of March 2002. It was already dead when discovered and described "like a primate" about the size like a large dog. The whole body, apart from feet and face, was covered in fur. It had a long tail. There are three versions about what happened with the corpse: The teacher Jakob Potapov from the neighboring settlement Borulakh said that the body had been taken to the capital Yakutsk. Someone else claimed that the animal had been torn to pieces by dogs and the third version was that "frightened people" had buried the corpse together with the trap.

The chief of the Sartan town council, Sergej Slepzov, talked about another similar case half a year earlier. A young man, Albert Slepzov, had found by coincidence a dead unknown animal which was similar to an ape. In this connection it was suggested that it could be a Chuchunaa as the 'wild man' are known in the region. Older local people who had seen the dead animal called it Aabasi kiila.

The reporter Elena Tikhonova and the photographer Michael Kotschetov contacted the relatives of Albert Slepzov in the settlement Badagaj. These confirmed that Slepzov had found a strange animal but were unable to say what happened with the corpse. However, according to the council workers of the Verkhoyansk region, Albert Slepzov´s father had buried the body. On hearing this the reporters started out from the capital Yakutsk to find Albert Slepzov in the Verkhoyansk region. After two hours flying time and twelve hour car driving on dirt tracks they arrived in the village Junkur where Albert Slepzov was supposed to be but wasn´t.

After various difficulties had been overcome, they were able to find the eyewitness's 64 year old father, Afanasi Slepzov, in another place. He reported that his son had found an unknown animal with a long tail in a trap at the end of the October 2001. The color of the coat was an unusual yellow. The boy was afraid and left the animal behind in the wilderness. Back at home he made a sketch of his find. After a few days Afanasi Slepzov tried to find the animal with a companion but, according to him, unsuccessfully due to new snowfall.

The reporters confronted Slepzov with the statements of other people in the village that in reality he had found the animal and had hidden it. Slepzov denied this. The questioning was not continued as it was obvious that the subject made him uncomfortable. According to statements of other village residents, Slepzov had initially kept his sons discovery secret and had first begun to talk about it when rumors were already circulating in the village. It was not possible for the reporters to visit the scene of the second finding in March 2002. Some time later a Moscow travel agency offered to finance another expedition.

The place where this happened lies on the arctic circle in the autonomous Republic of Sakha (Yakutia), eastern Siberia, with the capital Yakutsk about 200 kilometers east of the main ridge of the Verkhoyansk mountains. This area is one of the coldest on Earth where the winter temperature can fall to minus 70°C. It is possible to reach many settlements only by air or over roads which are passable only at certain times of the year. This makes the Chuchunaa one of the most difficult cryptids in the world to reach.

The Evidence

No physical evidence of the Chuchunaa has been brought forward to modern society. There are specific accounts of sightings which resulted in the beast being killed however no physical evidence has been able to support these claims. Evidence does however exist in the form of a photograph that can not be documented or dated. That photograph is found in our gallery.

The Sightings

• There were tales of a strange being wandering the remote forests of Tunguska near the scenes of devastation. The nomadic reindeer herdsmen of Siberia sighted the gigantic gray humanoid figure some 50 miles north of the Chunya river. They saw the man, who seemed to be over 8 feet in height, picking berries and drinking water from a stream. The superstitious Mongol herdsmen regarded the freakish-looking stranger as one of the fabled Chuchunaa. Others who supposedly investigated one of man kinds greatest mysteries "the Tunguska blast" have also claimed to have seen the Chuchunaa.

• Previous to 1928 both sightings and stories regarding the Chuchunaa were not common play but certainly widespread enough to be passed down through time and have the stories make their way into modern cities.

• In 1928, the Soviet government sent expeditions into the upper regions of the Indigirka and Yana rivers in order to collect accounts of these unique man-beasts. They documented a handful of sightings.

• Some old people claimed that in 1957 hunters from the surrounding villages killed a Chuchunaa, the snowman. It is said that its body was brought on the Lena river to Yakutsk [capital of Yakutia] and disappeared there.

• Many claim the last "reliable sightings" of the Chuchunaa came out of Siberia in the 1950s. Many speculate the sightings slowed because the grasp the Soviet Union had on the entire region during the cold war.

• Afanasi Slepzov reported that in October 2001 his son had seen an unusual animal with a yellow colored coat. It was described as a primate. The relationship between Afanasi and Albert Slepzov has not been confirmed but the stories seem to line up as father and son.

• In 2001 Albert Slepzov, had found by coincidence a dead unknown animal which was similar to an ape. In this connection it was suggested that it could be a Chuchunaa 3 as the 'wild man' are known in the region. He would not state what became of the body. • In a village in the Verkhoyansk region, Barylas district, an unknown animal had been caught in a wolf-trap in the middle of March 2002. It was described just as most of the Chuchunaa descriptions are. The body vanished one way or another. The story is above.

The Stats

• Classification: Primate or Neanderthal Man

• Size: 6 to 7 feet tall

• Weight: Heavy set body, probably 400-600lbs.

• Diet: Reports indicate these creatures are pillagers and eat as humans would

• Location: Siberia, Russia

• Movement: Walking

• Environment: Mountains, snow plains, Siberian forests

Chapter 13: Yeti

     The Yeti, also known as the Abominable Snowman or the Meteh Kangmi is a large humanoid creature thought to dwell in the Himalayan Mountains. Mainstream science considers the Yeti as nothing more than a hoax or misidentification of an already known species, but those who have seen the Yeti have a much different belief. The Western name Yeti is derived from the Tibetan word Yeh-Teh, which translates into "little man-like animal". It is a false cognate with Old English geottan, or yettin in modern English, which is an antiquated word for an orc or troll. In the Sherpa language, the word Yeti actually means "That there thing".

In 1921 the name Abominable Snowman was coined by British Lieutenant Colonel Charles Kenneth Howard-Bury. While leading "The Everest Reconnaisance" group on the Lhakpa La in the Mount Everest region, Howard-Bury's team discovered strange footprints at about 20,000 feet up. When Howard-Bury returned to Calcutta he described his sighting to Henry Newman, a reporter for The Statesman. While documenting the story, Newman mistranslated the word Metoh from the full name Metch Kangmi, the words the Sherpas had used to describe the creature, Metch meaning dirty, filthy or disgusting and Kangmi meaning man of the snow. Instead of translating the name Metch as he should he translated the word Metoh which was mistranslated into abominable.

So what about the 'abominable snowman' is so abominable? Perhaps it's the idea of something so close to us intellectually yet so different physically. Maybe it's the brute force suggested by relatively scarce tales. Quite possibly, it might be the idea that we, humanity, have areas to conquer that are ruled by beasts such as this. The idea of an animal of this form certainly makes us uneasy. Or maybe it's the chilling environment within which it resides: The Himalayas are as famous for their sheer size as they are for this beast that lurks amidst their peaks. The mountain chain has a length of about 2,400 kilometers and a width about 200 to 400 kilometers. Numerous peaks protrude into the sky at over 7,600 meters, one of them being the famed Mount Everest. These measurements are constantly being rendered obsolete as the mountains continue to rise every year as India impels into Nepal. When one considers the remoteness and size of this region of the earth, it does seem conceivable for a large creature, such as the reputed 'abominable snowman' to roam about the valleys, woods, crevices, and peaks of this behemoth mountain chain and elude humanity.

The Yeti has become a tourist attraction, although not to the extent of its North American cousin, Sasquatch. A person can sleep in the Yak & Yeti hotel or luxuriate in a warm meal at the Yeti bar, and get there by flying Yeti Airlines. But above 1,336 meters, commercialism ends and the bare truth takes over: frigid wind, immeasurable snow, absolute isolation, and the possibility of a wild, hairy hominid watching you from around some frozen bend. The Yeti seems to avoid people more than people attempt to avoid it. Perhaps that is why it is so experienced at parrying mankind.

For thousands of years, the legend of the Yeti remained confined to its remote area, where it is worshiped, inscribed in scrolls, and represented in the annual Mani Rimdu Festival. The Yeti is vaguely mentioned in the older days, perhaps first by Alexander the Great when his unrestrained sights fell on the Indus Valley. He would have liked to be presented with one, but the native people told him that the creature was unable to breathe properly at lower altitudes. In 79 A.D., Pliny the Elder wrote in his Natural History about creatures, living "in the Land of the Satyrs", that are swift and able to run on two and four feet. They had "human-like bodies, and because of their swiftness can only be caught when they are ill or old." After various other small odds and ends of information, Aelianus in his Animal Stories wrote: "If one enters the mountains neighboring India one comes upon lush, overgrown valleys. The Indians call this region Koruda. Animals that look like the Satyrs roam these valleys. They are covered with shaggy hair and have a long horse's tail When left to themselves they stay in the forest and eat tree sprouts. But when they hear the din of approaching hunters and the barking of dogs, they run with incredible speed to hide in the mountain caves. For they are masters at mountain climbing. They also repel approaching humans by hurling stones down at them."

The first time this creature was publicized in the Western world was some period within the 1800s by British military and Indian Civil Service. B.H. Hodgson had been in Nepal from 1820 to 1843, working at the Nepalese court. The British resident mentioned that his porters had, much to their fright, encountered a hairy, tail-less Wildman in northern Nepal. It was in the year of 1889 that more of the story spread to the west. At the time, unaccompanied western explorers seeking the culture and beauty of the Himalayas had to cloak themselves as wayfarers or nomadic tradesmen. It is in that very year that footprints were first reported in Major L. A. Waddell's book, Among the Himalayas.

Northeast of Sikkim, he had stumbled upon a trail of large footprints in the snow at 5,000 meters. His porters informed him of the Yeti and their belief that it left the footprints in the snow. Waddell dismissed this wild claim, and it was his belief that they were merely tracks of the red snow bear that resides in the region, Ursus isabellinus.

Soon, however, Tibet started to allow outsiders into this secluded region, and numerous expeditions set out to conquer Everest. And as they did so, the Yeti became a worldwide sensation with more evidence surfacing. The first attempts to climb the northward face of

Everest, by Lt.-Col. C. K. Howard-Bury also succeeded in sighting mysterious black figures in the distance. When he and his companions reached the spot on September 22, 1921, conveniently located at 7000 meters, they found enormous footprints, those of the alleged Metoh Kangmi.

In 1925, N.A. Tombazi, a photographer and member of the Royal Geographical Society, saw a creature at about 15,000 ft near Zemu Glacier. Tombazi witnessed this humanoid figure, wandering about in an upright fashion while leading an expedition to the South Glaciers of Kangchenjunga in the Sikkim Himalaya. He witnessed the strange creature pause to tug on dwarf rhododendron bushes as it passed, its dark figure casting extreme contrast to the white snow. Wearing no clothing the creature was easily distinguishable, any more observations of the beast where cut short as the creature moved into some thick brush and disappeared. Tombazi would later write: "...a couple of hours later, during the descent, I purposely made a detour so as to pass the place where the 'man' or 'beast' had been seen. I examined the footprints, which were clearly visible on the surface of the snow. They were similar in shape to those of a man, but only six to seven inches (15 to 17 cm) long by four inches (23 cm) wide at the broadest part of the foot. The marks of five distinct toes and the instep were perfectly clear, but the trace of the heel was indistinct, and the little that could be seen of it appeared to narrow down to a point. I counted fifteen such footprints at regular intervals ranging from one-and-a-half to two feet (30 to 45 cm). The prints were undoubtedly of a biped, the order of the spoor having no characteristics whatever of any imaginable quadruped. Dense rhododendron scrub prevented any further investigations as to the direction of the footprints..."

30 years later, the famed Eric Shipton had his first encounter with the creature's trails. Accompanying him were Michael Ward and Sen Tensing. The tracks they found were located within the Gauri Sankar range, not far from Everest itself, a location Shipton had previously attempted to climb five times.

The tracks stretched for about 1600 meters, dodging about and between crevasses, and eventually ending in a moraine. The tracks set about in this pattern measured thirty centimeters long. To display this oddity, Shipton laid down his pickax adjacent to one of the prints and snapped one of the most famous photographs representing this animal. From the picture, and Shipton's description, one can discern the big toe easily, for it is separated from the other three. One cannot be sure whether there are three or four other toes, two toes held together closely can seemingly merge into one when imprinted on the snow. Assuming that this is indeed some form of ape, five toes seems more plausible.

As mentioned, Shipton and his companions followed the tracks to their end in the moraine. But could it be that they were led into the wrong direction by assuming that the directions that the toes pointed is forward? That sentence might have sounded peculiar at first, but one must take into account many reports of the animal's bizarre manner of walking and gait with tendency to walk with its toes facing backward and heel facing forward. Curiously, many reports mention this detail. This method of walking can also be found in the Orang pendek, another hominoid like creature reputed to roam the jungles of Sumatra. There, however, the backward-step description is much more prominent. Within Megasthene's Inica, one can find the line, "In the mountains called Nulo there are men whose feet point backwards and have eight toes on the ends."

The 'eight toes' is something mentioned scarcely by Sherpas, and can easily be ruled out. No tracks with such deformities have been found, nor have any reports included this feature. Bears, although they don't have eight toes, do have a tendency to turn their toes inward and heels outward. Also, the Bear's small toe is actually the largest, and thus can be mistaken. When one looks down at their own foot, they would notice that the line of the foot slopes from the big toe down to the small toe. This is not consistent with the footprints photographed by Eric Shipton, however. There the line slopes downward from the small toes to the big toe, thus implying that the big toe is actually the small toe. It might be helpful to recite the preceding tongue twister several times so it can be fully understood. Needless to say, Shipton's photographs have proven very controversial.

The following account was published in the November 2, 1921 edition of The Times. It follows the account of Englishman William Knight, this being four years prior to Tombazi's encounter. He was returning from Tibet, in the Gangtok area, when he saw a beast much like a man, who was "...a little under 6 ft, 1.8 meters, high, almost stark naked in that bitter cold, it was the month of November. He was a kind of pale yellow all over, about the color of a Chinaman, a shock of matted hair on his head, little hair on his face, highly splayed feet, and large, formidable hands. His muscular development in the arms, thighs, legs and chest was terrific. He had in his hand what seemed to be some form of primitive bow."

This is not the only encounter hinting at the possibility of tool usage and relatively eminent mentality. Jean Marques-Riviere told of his encounter in L'Inde Secrete et sa Magie. There, he tells how he joined a band of Nepalese men who informed him of footprints found and an armed expedition was to go in search of there creator. He joined the group and they trekked the "jungle 3 meters high". Then, several days after their initial start, a continual, repetitive rumbling sound broke the silence. As the group drew nearer to the source of the echoing sound, the prints of "snowmen" fell besides their own, and the group scattered. Finally, only three men were willing to move onward, one of them being Marques-Riviere.

"We went forward cautiously; the noise grew louder. Suddenly, one of us made a sign to stop and look. In front of us, in a natural circle of high rocks, among the huge hunks of broken stone, an extraordinary spectacle met our eye; some ten giant ape-men, 3 to 4 meters high, were gathered in a ring. One of them was beating a primitive tom-tom made of a hollow tree-trunk. The man's strength must have been terrific to judge by the noise he was making. The others swayed silently in time with the tom-tom. It was some religious ceremony, no doubt, for their solemn manner and attitude showed that they were performing a magic rite. Their bodies were covered with hair and their faces were halfway between a gorilla's and a man's. But there was nothing of the animal about their attitude, and the one that was beating the tom-tom stood upright like a human being. They were quite naked, in spite of the bitter cold in this desolate region and a strange sadness could be seen on their frightful faces."

The tale does not stop there, but proceeds into the author questioning the creature's existence. Readers can draw one conclusion about these tales: although often romanticized, these stories do have some root in reality. But how precisely can this reality be defined?

Yellow skin below matted hair, extremely robust body, cone-shaped head, and an oddly human stance, this is the common description of the Yeti. As with most crypto zoological beings, people have attempted to link it with a presumed extinct prehistoric animal, and have succeeded in doing so. The similarities between the Yeti and what is known as Gigantopithecus blacki is almost uncanny. This giant ape, with proportions that coincide with those of the Yeti, was discovered by Ralph Von Koenigswald in the unlikeliness of places: a jar full of teeth in a Chinese medicine shop. Later, a jawbone of this beast was found in a Chinese cave, one of the same caves that are reputed to hold another hairy hominid, the Yeren. When compared with the jaw of a gorilla, the true proportions of this monstrous creature are clearly shown.

As with all extinct creatures, we can only speculate to its true appearance. 3 and 4 meters high, standing on its hind legs, the creature must have been a terror to all animals scurrying about in the Middle Pleistocene period. But, do we really have to speculate, or can we perhaps simply look for the Yeti?

Gigantopithecus was not the only giant ape to have seemingly disappeared thousands of years ago. Pithecanthropus erectus, officially announced in 1894, was at first, considered the 'Missing Link.' Ralph Von Koenigswald, who originally discovered the teeth of Gigantopithecus, organized a three-year expedition to excavate more ape-men in 1936. Shortly after the expedition began the team discovered a new ape creature. It bore much similarity to the Pithecanthropus, yet was given its own genus, Sinanthropus. This discovery happened in Peking, this could mean it is possible that ape men such as this were spread throughout Asia at the time, and may still be thriving in isolated groups. These are smaller than the average Yeti, yet could account for one of the three groups of Yetis, as will later be discussed.

After his finds of Pithecanthropus, Ralph Von Koenigswald proceeded onward to find yet another ape, this time considerably larger. It was christened Meganthropus palaeojavanicus. The jawbone, the only remains of this beast, seemed more human than those of the Gigantopithecus, and about a quarter smaller, but still titanic in comparison to the modern apes and Homo sapiens. Meganthropus' proportions were similar to those of Gigantopithecus, with an estimated height of 3 meters.

Then again, who said that the Yeti had to be some form of extinct creature at all? Consistent with some suspicious footprints, it is entirely plausible that the Yeti is a common black bear. Reinhold Messner holds that belief after researching the topic first hand, as documented in his book, My Quest for the Yeti. According to him, the idea of the Yeti to the locals is that of a 'man bear.' Messner himself sighted a yeti on two separate occasions, the second of which he was pursued in the darkness and sought refuge in a local village. But after witnessing a bear in the act of running on two legs, he became convinced that the Yeti phenomenon could be fully accounted for by taking in the possibility of the snowman being a mere Ursus. This idea should not be disappointing, if it is indeed true. A new species of bear would also be quite provoking, although perhaps not as stirring as a giant ape further up on the evolutionary ladder.

As more and more cases are examined, the Yeti does start to hold uncanny resemblance to simple bears. Big, hairy, hulking, and with an omnivorous diet it does point in a definite and possible direction, though one that slips through the general publics fingers because of its lack of romance. In a letter to Messner, the German explorer and zoologist Erns Schäfer wrote that in 1934 he had gone in search of the Himalayan beast, hoping to bring back a male and female exemplar, and in Inner Tibet he managed to shoot "a number of Yetis, in the form of the mighty Tibetan bear, Ursus thibetanus." He claimed that Shipton and Smythe had asked him not to publish his findings so that they would still receive funding for their next Everest expedition. Could it be that Tombazi, Messner, Knight, Waddell, and all others have been describing a bear?

There are a number of bears that reside in this region. The Asiatic or Tibetan black bear has a wide range that reaches from Iran to Russia to Japan and is known to live in the Himalayas. These animals have long, black fur, particularly around the shoulders and throat. They have large ears and a white patch across their chests. These omnivorous mammals live up to 25 years and males have been known to reach up to 200 kilograms in weight. The interesting part is that they are known to be aggressive toward man and tend to stand on their back legs when frightened or aggravated. And because of their amazing ability to stand on their hind legs, they are often trained to dance as cubs for amusement. This is perhaps the likeliest candidate for the Yeti should it actually be a bear..

Among the snow leopards and yaks, and behind the black bear there is also the brown bear, having many similar characteristics in its size and longevity. Of all the bears on earth, this particular species has the widest range and can be found in Europe, Asia, and America. In the countries surrounding Nepal, they are listed as endangered. Still, could such a widespread species be held accountable for all the sightings, furs, and prints left in the snow? If not, then there is always the Tibetan blue bear, one of the rarest specimens from the Ursus genus. And lastly, there is the Himalayan red bear, Ursus isabellinus, After examining these animals, it is clear that there are quite a bit of big, hairy, and hulking things in the Himalayas besides the reputed Yeti, ones that could turn out to be the famed 'Abominable Snowman.'

Messner's encounters do have quite a bit of resemblance to other sightings and the fact that he became convinced that it was simply a bear shows that it may very well be that way. At the sight of one bear running away on two legs, Messner said that it "looked uncannily like a wild man." The only factor to counter this is that the lamas and Sherpas know the region well and yet they are the ones convinced that the Yeti is more than a simple mashiung, or bear. For them, the black bears are a totally separate animal. One would think that the local and nomadic people occupying the region would be familiar with the local fauna. But there will always be skeptics. The sighting Messner later attributed to a bear goes as follows: "Making my way through some ash-colored juniper bushes, I suddenly heard an eerie sound¾a whistling noise, similar to the warning call mountain goats make. Out of the corner of my eye I saw the outline of an upright figure dart between the trees to the edge of the clearing, where low-growing thickets covered the steep slope. The figure hurried on, silent and hunched forward, disappearing behind a tree only to reappear again against the moonlight. It stopped for a moment and turned to look at me. Again I heard the whistle, more of an angry hiss, and for a heartbeat I saw eyes and teeth. The creature towered menacingly, its face a gray shadow, its body a black outline. Covered with hair, it stood upright on two short legs and had powerful arms that hung down almost to its knees. I guessed it to be over seven feet tall. Its body looked much heavier than that of a man of that size, but it moved with such agility and power toward the edge of the escarpment that I was both startled and relieved. Mostly I was stunned. No human would have been able to run like that in the middle of the night. It stopped again beyond the trees by the low-growing thickets, as if to catch its breath, and stood motionless in the moonlit night without looking back."

The famous Austrian mountain climber knew the Himalayas well and had trekked across the region over fifty separate times since 1970. His questions to the Sherpas yielded many different answers, but none supported the Yeti being something with the likeness of a hominid. All the stories of the Yeti have become garbled and indefinite with truth diluted in a gigantic mass of rumors and fictional tales put together for tourists. In the mind of the natives, the Yeti is no definite thing that is there. It is beyond material, a more spiritual being. People in Tibet hold an indefinite line between that which is true and that which is spiritual. Still, sacrifices are still made in Nepal to the mystical beast before men leave villages for the hunt. In Tibet, however, Buddhism does not permit for such killings.

One of the things that perplex researchers about these creatures and the footprints they leave in their wake is the altitude at which they are found. Upwards of 6000 meters, it is rare to see anything but a bird. There are animals that live above this line, but they lead an active lifestyle where they descend into the woods below daily in search of food. It is possible that the Yeti is some form of ape that we already are familiar with, yet has adapted to its frigid environment. As Dr. Bernard Heuvelmans mentions in his book, On the Track of Unknown Animals, it is possible for an ape, such as on orang-utan for instance, to resort to walking on its hind legs so it has less area touching the icy snow beneath. Orang-utans are even known to have once lived in the foothills of the Himalayas.

It is also possible that, just as some of its animal neighbors, the Yeti lives at the higher altitudes, only to descend into the woods below for food. One can imagine that this is quite exhausting, especially in the harsh conditions of the Himalayas, but apparently, creatures do manage to sustain a lifestyle in this manner. According to Charles Stonor and the other men confined within his group, this creature fed upon the small, mouse-like creatures, marmots and pikas that thrive amidst the rocks. This statement was based on a combination of information from the natives and actual animal droppings, the latter of which two discoveries were made. Oddly, mixed in with the animal fur and bones was earth, present for unknown reasons. Some natives added juvenile yaks, tahr, musk deer, and birds and their eggs to the menu.

Another possibility is that the Yeti, when sighted at these altitudes is simply passing across the snowy peaks to get from one valley to another. In the woods below, one could walk within several meters of this beast and not know it, save for the smell. But in the vast, white, and open expanses of the snowy peaks and tilted plains above, the dark-haired creature is hard to miss. This theory may explain why most sightings occur there as well.

Yet it is possible that none of these ordinary and other long gone beasts can account for the sightings of the 'yeh-teh'. Sightings and folklore divide the Yeti phenomenon into three distinct groups.

The mih-teh, meaning 'a man-like living thing that is not a human being.', is the most commonly mentioned Yeti. When one refers to the giant ape creature with the sloping forehead and the enormous feet, they are speaking about the mi-teh, or the meh-teh. This is considered dangerous, especially in comparison with the two other types. The creature's description can be compiled into that of a stocky ape-man with an eerie human quality to it. Short, coarse reddish-brown to black in color hair runs down especially at the shoulders. Amidst the hair is the robust face with large teeth and mouth. A conical head, certainly a notable feature, is also described.

The second type of Yeti is the dzu-teh, 'a hulking thing.' The creature is not dangerous in any way to man, and it is the largest of the Yetis. It is reputed to lead an omnivorous diet and to walk on four and two legs, leading many people to believe that it is no more than the common black bear, as discussed above.

And lastly, there is the teh-lma, a third type of Yeti discerned from folklore and tales by Gerald Russell. This Yeti is quite different from the other two, being a little less than a meter high at its peak age, about 45 centimeters at earlier stages. It is nocturnal, and it cannot be ruled out that the mih-teh and the dzu-teh are nocturnal as well. While the other Yetis are seen at dizzying heights, this creature is said to thrive within the forests below, stalking frogs among other creatures under the shroud of night. Being much smaller than the other Yetis does not alter the creature's amazing strength, for this beast too is reputed to hold immense vigor.

As with most expeditions that set out to search for crypto zoological creatures, be it in the African Congo or in the Himalayas, the search for the Yeti has turned up little evidence to hold up the heavy weight supported by its believers. The most excitement in a typical expedition comes from a track of footprints across the snow. Although exhilarating to consider what kind of creature made them, they are not anything new and unprecedented in science, with hundreds of different cases documenting these inexplicable impressions in the snow.

It is not quite clear who first set foot upon the peak of Everest, Sir Edmund Hillary or Tensing Norgay. It is clear, however, that on the way there and back, Hillary gathered tales about the mysterious creature, the Yeti, and found him immersed in it later on. This would also lead to the examination of the controversial and elusive yeti scalp.

Perhaps the most interesting, and questionable as mentioned above, evidence for the Yeti came in 1953. On October 9th, Rusy Gandhy, J. A. Gaitonde, P. V. Pattankar, and Navnit Parekh stopped at the Pangboche monastery. There, the four mountaineers were informed of the presence of a sacred object, the scalp of the mountain man within the walls of the local gompa. Reluctantly, they were shown the scalp, along with Professor Christoph Von Furer-Haimendorf, who conveniently happened to be a passing anthropologist, and Dr. Charles Evans.

Indeed, the scalp does fit the description of the Yeti, with a conical shape and long hairs running down the side, while the top is bald. One can assume that this is not a trait of age in the being itself, but rather, the fact of a long dead creature, from which the scalp was detached.

The problem lay at the scalp's purpose, an object of sacred worship. In its absence, bad luck would be bestowed upon the monastery and its inhabitants. No bad luck came from reducing the scalp's hair to one less, and the single hair was sent of to Dr. Leon A. Hausman in New Jersey.

On an expedition funded by the Daily Mail, the discovery of a second scalp in Khumjung had everyone involved hopefully to prove the creature's existence. When examined, the two scalps both bore similar characteristics, and as experts would note, they were made of a single piece of skin. Sadly, the same can't be said for a third scalp in Namche Bazar. Either the scalp had not properly been removed from the beast atop which it once resided, or more likely, it was no more than an imitation. Could jealousy lead natives to fake a sacred object? Perhaps it was indeed fabricated long ago and over the course of time people forgot its falsified origin and genuinely began to believe in its authenticity. Whatever the case may be this indeed raised doubt in the other objects' genuineness.

Another expedition to seek the Yeti set out in 1957. Tom Slick, with a successful career in the oil industry and a taste for the mysterious, pushed forth the expedition for the next three years, over the course of the expedition many hairs where sent in for examination. And accompanying the tale of the scalp with which they returned is the bones of what is reputed to be a Yeti. They were discovered by Peter Byrne within the Pangboche monastery. The bones seem rather small, especially in contrast with the scalp. They, too, are very controversial, partially due to the manner in which they were obtained. Mr. Byrne, for the sake of science and curiosity, ended up having to lead one of the monastery caretakers to drunkenness just so he could switch the bones of the Yeti with those of a man. Rather than proving anything with this act, Byrne only complicated the situation. Primates do have comparatively small hands, but the bones are no bigger than those of a human. They affirm nothing, and could very well be human.

Then, a Japanese expedition went looking for the Yeti. Leading it was Dr. Teizo Ogawa of Tokyo University. It comes as no surprise that, after examining the scalps, more hairs were taken. From all of these hair samples, the creature's identity could not be revealed, but one thing was true: all three scalps, even the one made of patches, had the same hairs interpolated into their skin. So, they had come from the same animal, whether a bulky, hominid ape, or some harmless forest-dwelling creature.

At the time of examination, technology was not at the level it is today; thus analysis could not be taken further. However, with new technologies and developments, startling new evidence has come about. For the moment, however, scientist could only put it beneath the objective of a microscope and compare it with hairs from other known animals. Although the scientist did not find a scapegoat to point to, they did eliminate all possible animals within the Himalayas, as well as a wide range of other mammals from the far corners of the globe. Dr. Hausman's skepticism leads him to believe that the skin was brought from some travelers or tourists, being some animal from some other country, and was left there.

Also, because of the arrangement and direction of the hairs, it is not possible to have come from another animal's back, the most likely origin of the skin if Dr. Hausman is correct. The largest portion of unvarying skin can be found on an animal's hind. All of this speculation and mystery led Sir Edmund Hillary to go in attempt to persuade the natives to lend the scalp temporarily while it is examined in detail. After much debating, the locals gave in and the scalp was sent off to Chicago, where it would be forwarded to Paris, and lastly to London. After extensive examination, the scalp was labeled as the 200-year-old skin of the serow, a goat-like creature that is indeed present in the Himalayas. Yeti or not, when returned, the scalp was yet again placed as the monastery's sacred object.

So the scalp, not proven authentic or fake, still rests confined within the walls of the monastery, gathering dust and loosing valuable hairs that could be equated to one of the greatest discoveries of our time. But the series of rumored anatomical remains of Yetis was not limited to hands and scalps. In other monasteries, furs and even an entire 400-year-old mummified corpse have been found. Thorough examination of all of them has not turned up any startling evidence. The mummy's hands were supported by sticks rather than bones. But do these invalid specimens imply that the entire Yeti myth is false?

At the turn of the century, a new startling discovery was made. A British expedition set out in search of this elusive creature when mysterious hairs were found in the hollow of a cedar tree in the eastern Bhutan area. Naturally, the hairs were carefully removed in a forensic manner and flown back to Britain.

"We found some DNA in it, but we don't know what it is. It's not a human, not a bear nor anything else we have so far been able to identify. It's a mystery and I never thought this would end in a mystery. We have never encountered DNA that we couldn't recognize before."

This is the analysis set forth by Bryan Spykes, a Professor of Human Genetics at the Oxford Institute of Molecular Medicine.

And so it remains to this day, shrouded in a riddle with insufficient material. With all this supporting evidence, and amounting physical evidence, it seems that we have not really excelled much farther than from the times that the Western world first heard of this enchanting tale. If there is indeed a bulky, hairy bipedal hominid roaming the remote valleys and woods of Nepal and Tibet, it is possible that it will elude science for many years to come. Or perhaps, its discovery is right around the corner. Then again, the entire Yeti phenomenon may be nothing more than our imaginations running wild. Odd things can happen at high altitudes where air is icy and thin. But if discovered, the mountain men will simply be added to the tree of life and to wildlife databases, and then forgotten like the mountain gorillas and the Komodo dragons that inspired tales just as riveting as the Yeti.

The Evidence

Unlike most Cryptid creatures the Yeti actually has a wealth of physical evidence, but does this evidence support the Yeti's existence or disprove it as an already known species. Like its American counterpart, Yeti footprints are the most common form of evidence that suggests something large and unknown has recently walked through the snow. Perhaps the strangest bit of evidence as brought back to London hidden in the suitcase of actor Jimmy Stewart in 1959.

Although it has never been determined exactly what creature the hand once belonged to, a picture of the famed hand is now on display at Disney Land in promotion of their new ride, Expedition Everest. There are also scalps which reportedly belong to the Yeti, used as sacred artifacts in local monasteries these scalps are rarely available for testing. However a hair sample was obtained and when tested did not match any know creature. On top of all of this physical evidence, credible sightings of the creature have been reported since modern man first began to explore the region.

The Sightings

In 1832, the Journal of the Asiatic society of Bengal published the account of B. H. Hodgson, who wrote that while trekking in northern Nepal, his native guides spotted a tall, bipedal creature covered with long dark hair, then fled in fear. Hodgson did not see the creature, but concluded it was an orangutan. An early record of reported footprints appeared in 1889 in L.A. Waddell's Among the Himalayas He reported his native guides described a large apelike creature that left the prints, but concluded the prints were made by a bear. Waddell heard stories of bipedal, apelike creatures, but wrote that of the many witnesses he questioned, none "could ever give me an authentic case. On the most superficial investigation it always resolved into something that somebody had heard of." The frequency of reports increased in the early 20th century, when Westerners began making determined attempts to climb the many mountains in the area and sometimes reported seeing odd creatures or strange tracks.

In 1925, N.A. Tombazi, a photographer and member of the Royal Geographical Society, saw a creature at about 15,000 ft near Zemu Glacier. Tombazi later wrote that he observed the creature from about 200 or 300 yards, for about one minute. "Unquestionably, the figure in outline was exactly like a human being, walking upright and stopping occasionally to pull at some dwarf rhododendron bushes. It showed up dark against the snow, and as far as I could make out, wore no clothes." About two hours later, Tombazi and his companions descended the mountain, and saw what they took to be the creature's prints, described as "similar in shape to those of a man, but only six to seven inches long by four inches wide.... The prints were undoubtedly those of a biped."

In the 1950s, Slawomir Rawicz in a book ghostwritten by British reporter Ronald Dowling claimed that he had seen two large, apelike creatures while crossing the Himalaya in 1942. He claimed to have observed the creatures for several hours from a distance of about 100 m

(109 yards). However, Rawicz's claim is now considered to be a hoax and it has been proven that he was never in the Himalayas in 1942.

Western interest in the yeti peaked dramatically in the 1950s. While attempting to scale Mount Everest in 1951, Eric Shipton took photographs of a number of large prints in the snow, at about 6,000 m (19,685 ft) above sea level. These photos have been subject to intense study and debate. Some argue they are the best evidence of Yeti's reality, but others contend the prints are from a mundane creature and have been distorted and enlarged by the melting snow.

In 1953, Sir Edmund Hillary and Tenzing Norgay reported seeing large footprints while scaling Mount Everest. Hillary would later discount yeti reports as unreliable. During the Daily Mail Abominable Snowman Expedition of 1954, the largest search of its kind, the mountaineering leader John Angelo Jackson, made the first trek from Everest to Kangchenjunga and in the process photographed symbolic paintings of the yeti at Thyangboche Gompa. Jackson tracked and also photographed many footprints in the snow, many of which were identifiable. However, there were many large footprints which could not be identified. The flattened footprint like indentations were attributed to erosion and subsequent widening of the original footprint by wind and particle action.

Beginning in 1957, Tom Slick, an American who had made a fortune in oil, funded a few missions to investigate yeti reports. In 1959, feces reportedly from a yeti were collected by Slick's expedition. Analysis found a parasite but could not classify it. Bernard Heuvelmans wrote that "Since each animal has its own parasites, this indicated that the host animal is equally an unknown animal."

In 1959, actor Jimmy Stewart, while visiting India, reportedly smuggled the remains of a supposed yeti, the so-called Pangboche Hand, by hiding them in his luggage when he flew from India to London.

In 1960, Sir Edmund Hillary mounted an expedition to collect and evaluate evidence for the yeti and sent a yeti scalp from the Khumjung monastery to the West for testing. The results indicated that the scalp had been manufactured from the skin of the serow, a goat-like Himalayan antelope. But some disagreed with this analysis. Shackley said they "pointed out that hairs from the scalp look distinctly monkey-like, and that it contains parasitic mites of a species different from that recovered from the serow."

In 1970, British mountaineer Don Whillans says he saw a creature while scaling Annapurna. While scouting for a campsite, Whillans heard some odd cries. His Sherpa guide told him the sound was a yeti's call. That night, reported Whillans, he saw a dark shape moving near his camp. The next day, Whillans observed a few human like footprints in the snow, and that evening, he asserted that with binoculars, he watched a bipedal, ape-like creature for about 20 minutes as it apparently searched for food not far from his camp.

The Stats

- Classification: Hominid

- Size: Most reports at about 9ft tall however smaller versions are reported too

- Weight: Unknown

- Diet: Varies from Mean to Local Plant Life

- Location: Himalayan Mountains

- Movement: Walking

- Environment: Snow Covered Mountains and Forest Rich Valleys

Lightning Source UK Ltd.
Milton Keynes UK
UKOW04f0625221017

311426UK00001B/54/P